THE SOUTHERN POETRY ANTHOLOGY

VOLUME VI

TENNESSEE

FIRST EDITION, 2013

Requests for permission to reproduce material from this work should be sent to:

Permissions
Texas Review Press
English Department
Sam Houston State University
Huntsville, TX 77341-2146

Cover design and photo by Chad M. Pelton

A brief word about the below information: The Library of Congress directed us to use the CIP data from the first volume of the anthology, even though we have distinct data for other volumes. The correct publication information is listed below, before this data:

Title: The Southern Poetry Anthology, VI: Tennessee
Editors: Jesse Graves, William Wright, and Paul Ruffin
ISBN-13: 978-1-937875-45-9

Library of Congress Cataloging-in-Publication Data

The Southern poetry anthology : South Carolina / [compiled] by Stephen Gardner and
William Wright — 1st ed.
    p. cm.
  ISBN-13: 978-1-933896-06-9 (pbk. : alk. paper)
  ISBN-10: 1-933896-06-X (pbk : alk. paper)
  1. American poetry–South Carolina. I. Gardner, Stephen. II. Wright, William, 1979-
  PS558.S6S68 2007
  811.008'09757–dc22
                    2007023711

THE SOUTHERN POETRY ANTHOLOGY

VOLUME VI

TENNESSEE

William Wright, *Series Editor*

Jesse Graves, Paul Ruffin, & William Wright, *Volume Editors*

The editors dedicate this volume
to the memories of
George Scarbrough and Steve Sparks

Foreword

The state of Tennessee is widely recognized as a home of great music, and its geographic regions are as distinct as Memphis blues, Nashville country, and Bristol old-time sounds. Virtually all of America's popular music has roots in the state. Tennessee's literary heritage offers just as broad an aesthetic and political compass, as home to both the Fugitive Agrarian Poets, with Allen Tate's "Ode to the Confederate Dead," as well as Nikki Giovanni's signature voice from the Black Arts Movement, whose poem "Knoxville, Tennessee" presents an African American family experience. Few places present such a rich multicultural spectrum as the Volunteer State.

The poems in *The Southern Poetry Anthology, Volume VI: Tennessee* engage the storied histories, diverse cultures, and vibrant rural, urban, and suburban landscapes of the state. Driving from Mountain City, in the northeast corner, to Memphis, in the southwest, would take roughly nine hours, starting out from some of the world's oldest mountains, deep in Appalachia, and ending up at a bridge to cross America's greatest river. One passes virtually everything in between the two cities, a continuing snapshot of the American panorama of mountain coves, small farms, national forests, blue-collar towns, eclectic cities, and sprawling metropolises.

Among the more than one hundred and twenty poets represented are Pulitzer and Bollingen Prize-winner Charles Wright, Brittingham Prize-winner Lynn Powell, and Agnes Lynch Starrett Prize-winners Kate Daniels, Rick Hilles, Bobby C. Rogers, and Arthur Smith. Alongside such widely known and celebrated poets are many writers at the very beginnings of promising literary lives, some of whom will go on to publish books and win awards of their own. One of the principal goals of this collection is to put the near future of Tennessee poetry on display beside the vitality of its present and the prominence of its past.

The book includes an introduction from renowned East Tennessee poet Jeff Daniel Marion, who in 1978 received the first literary fellowship from the Tennessee Arts Commission. No one has done more to shape the literature of Tennessee and the Appalachian region in general than Mr. Marion, and no one is better suited to connect the past, present, and future of Tennessee poetry. The editors hope that this timely anthology will stand for many years as the definitive poetic document for the great state of Tennessee.

Jesse Graves, Johnson City, TN
William Wright, Marietta, GA

Introduction

It is perhaps fitting that this anthology of Tennessee poetry appears almost one hundred years following the first meetings of a group in Nashville in 1914 who by 1922 came to be known as the Fugitives, a signal gathering highly influential in the course of early 20th century American poetry. In fact, Thomas Daniel Young in his 1981 critical study *Tennessee Writers* devotes an entire chapter to "The Fugitives" (John Crowe Ransom, Allen Tate, Robert Penn Warren, Donald Davidson, Merrill Moore, Ridley Wills, and others) but, with the notable exceptions of Randall Jarrell and George Scarbrough, finds little to almost no poetry to comment on following the Fugitives. Truth is, poetry was alive and well in Tennessee for some time, especially since the founding of the *Tennessee Poetry Journal* by Stephen Mooney in 1967 at the University of Tennessee at Martin, a journal that spanned only four years and twelve issues but whose influence directly and indirectly affected many of the poets in this current anthology.

In the 1960s and '70s, the "lifeblood" for poetry existed in the "little" magazines and journals, places where new writing was welcomed alongside the work of poets widely respected. In that time period, Tennessee was home not only to the *Tennessee Poetry Journal* in Martin, but also to *raccoon* in Memphis, *Vanderbilt Poetry Journal* in Nashville, *Puddingstone* in Knoxville, *The Small Farm* in Jefferson City, and the oldest continuously published journal in the United States, *The Sewanee Review*. All of these journals published poets within as well as outside Tennessee, with *Tennessee Poetry Journal*'s being a standard bearer with its stated credo: "Our purpose is to acquaint readers, particularly Tennesseans, with good poets from their own region and from the nation at large; to affirm the sense of place as a source of poetry; to bring those on the outside in, to send those on the inside out."

Listen to William Stafford writing about Tennessee nearly half a century ago in *Tennessee Poetry Journal* (Spring 1968):

THE TENNESSEE CIRCUIT

Sons of the statues in Tennessee
walk the town square.
Creeks run whiskey in the fall
to cheat the revenuer.
The color our country is braids out,

red, white, and blue, and gray—
the color hills return to after the fall,
before the spring campaign.

In Tennessee, you can hear events.
Listen along the track: someone
is talking in the parlor car,
posed for a whiskey ad:

"Now listen here; this is the way
I like to stand, posed in the parlor car,
proud of my country . . .
Just traveling through?"

Tennessee acts out more
of our nation than most states do:
lakes like the eyes of volunteers,
valleys neutral in the haze,
horses that walk into their own pictures,
children that loom like statues,
carrying history under their arms,
day by day, traveling through.

Now make your own circuit of Tennessee through this lively and widely ranging anthology of the poets whose imaginations live here, in this place and time, carrying history in their words. Don't miss Diann Blakely's take on "History" in contemporary Nashville, a South of "ranch-house Taras" and silver "bought at garage sales" or Gaylord Brewer's "Interruption: A Coyote in Tennessee" for its acute perceptions of this place's shifting inhabitants. Add to those Bill Brown's subtle commentary on a Tennessee poet's enduring challenge to name this world and its beings. Then listen to the new and promising voices of Catherine Childress in "Putting Up Corn" and Samuel Church in "Gift for Grandfather." What you'll find in your journey through these pages is *Tennessee the place* newly discovered, reinterpreted, deeply felt, sometimes with acceptance, sometimes not, and sometimes with ambivalence. Whatever the stance or attitude, here you'll find the work of nationally praised poets such as Charles Wright and Mark Jarman along with the new voice of Melissa Range, who turns a phrase from the past—"flat as a flitter"—into a subtle exposure of the horrors of mountaintop removal coal mining in her East Tennessee home community. Here's a poet who understands the irony and ambivalence involved in her Tennessee roots:

> "When you coming home?" my grandmother
> would ask on the phone, and how could I tell her
> that the crooked hills where we were born are my own
> true love and truer suffocation . . . .
> ("Crooked as a Dog's Hind Legs")

That, indeed, is the complex relationship you'll find as you make your circuit through this necessary, long overdue anthology of Tennessee's contemporary poets.

—Jeff Daniel Marion

Contents

Darnell Arnoult

Lining Out

I wrote a poem while I hung out clothes
this morning, but it left me.
My dryer's broken. I resort to the old ways,
outlawed now in fancy housing developments.
In the outlands, I sometimes see these young
girls' clothes hanging haphazard as their lives,
artless. No apprenticeship, only hard recourse
to troubled choices, their backless bloomers
flipping in the spring breeze for everyone to see.
That's not how it's done. Big things hang
on the ends and on the outside: sheets and towels
and bedspreads where the line's highest. Like my
grandmother's line, mine could stand some
maintenance. A lost art, hanging clothes. Too domestic
for poetry, some man once told me.
All whites go together. Colors hang separately.
Don't hang shirts by the shoulders. Pray for
sun on Mondays. Iron on Tuesdays.
The time my slow flawless hand went in the ringer
Granny's hand darted cross the air like a snake.
The way she hit the release scared me to death.
We carried wash up from the basement
in bright scarred metal dishpans to four slick bleached
white ropes waiting there like a skeleton holding
out for muscle. We hung and slapped straight
and pinched our sweet work in the shape of
our lives and waited for the sun to dry.

While You Are Away

for William

For days I count the dishes
and the glasses, the dresses
in the closet, the saucers
without cups, the pairs
of drugstore spectacles
that surprise me
as I move through the house—
each one evidence of your habits
and obsessions.
For hours
I finger the seat cushion,
pillow,
ashtray, door knob, faucet
at the back door that refuses to drip
dry. For minutes on end I pretend
that I float above the carpet,
some reverse magnetic hovering
principle at work, cooling, keeping
me above the floor,
keeping me from counting
my own footsteps
in any of these
empty rooms.

Hiding

Don't make me come looking for you.
Don't make me have to comb the house,
the car, the truck, the tractor, the back
of the toilet, the garage, the shed, the pile
of papers on the kitchen counter,
the crappy space beneath the couch cushions
where you've probably latched onto something
old and sticky, down inside the workings
of the recliner where God
knows some mouse is probably nesting
thinking of having babies.
Where else could you be?
I know you're watching me
like so many owls' eyes,
laughing from your comfortable perches
while I search high and low, inside and out.
Sure, chuckle as I move this and that,
swipe my fingers across the dust
I can't really see anymore without you.
Amuse yourselves while I stretch
my arms out as far as they'll go
trying to read the blessed phonebook.
How can you be so cruel? To wait
patiently in your hidey holes,
watching panic climb out my collar and
frustration cloud my memory all the more.
I've paid plenty for each of you,
but not so much that you can afford to be
coy, mean, mischievous. You aren't prescription,
you know. You're not official.
Your elitist attitude is only as good
as what I put in front of you
under a good light. So come out, come out,
wherever you are! For pity's sake,
make yourselves useful! Or I'll drive—
something I can still do without you
sonsabitches—to Dollar General
and lay down another
Abraham Lincoln
because you need to learn
anything, I mean anything,
can be replaced.

Beth Bachmann

Temper

Some things are damned to erupt like wildfire,
windblown, like wild lupine, like wings, one after
another leaving the stone-hole in the greenhouse glass.
Peak bloom, a brood of blue before firebrand.
And though it is late in the season, the bathers, also,
obey. One after another, they breathe in and butterfly
the surface: *mimic white, harvester, spot-celled sister,*
fed by the spring, the water beneath is cold.

Elegy

No shepherds. No nymphs. Maybe just one:
the girl the fawn strips like a fisherman's rose.
Death turns its mouth red. It can no longer lie
in the lilies. Not on my watch. The lake is filthy
with silver fish sticky with leeches. Lovesick,
I flick a feather into the water. No stones.
Only the one in my pocket, heavy as a tongue.

Jeff Baker

At Chota: Flooded Cherokee Capital

"... some of the tribes have become extinct and others have left but
remnants to preserve for awhile their once terrible names."
   —Andrew Jackson to Congress, 1829

The torched bush of the mind
Flickering out, thought
Flickering, becoming ash—
All night the lake read like a text
Written in watersnakes—
Bullfrogs, caught, sang
Death's language—foxfire,
Loosed breath of the drowned
Nation—whose ground we walk on—
What ground—whose laments we pray
Will not kindle—stripped bark
Of night—these waters pressing
Into—these red rocks
Quarried from the mountainside—
Seaside—Ordovician
Sediment broke upward
And America rose—glacial
Phosphate of dead sea animals—
Volcanic and eroding—
Utica mud shale—Trenton
Limestone—manifold cephalopods
And jawless fish-like vertebrates
Pressed in stone—preserved
Between the layers—locks
Of hair in a family Bible—
Confederates boxed in the stone—
Burial mounds troved
By the men of the state—
Tennessee Valley Authority—
Hydroelectric Lethe-waters—
Rank shimmer over the lost
Grounds—Sequoyah's syllabary's
Lost ash—Cherokee glottal
Ghost-music bubbling-up—

Surfacing snapping-turtles—
Vicious, lethargic, prehistoric—
Mind out—it seemed each sunrise
Pressed its dire eye to a keyhole,
Beyond which memory—Mother—
Rose from her youthful bath,
Loosening her terrible jaw—

Evelyn McAmis Bales

All That Remains

In the Toe River valley,
stacked stone foundation marks
where the homeplace once stood,
walls long returned to dust and humus.

In yard overgrown with weeds,
flat stones still lead
where front porch once rang
with story and song.

Inside crumbling springhouse walls,
creek mint covers stepping stones;
and moss claims the ledges
where crocks of sweet milk and butter cooled.

At twilight the stillness speaks here
of farmer come home to his rest,
of mother nursing a little one at her breast
while the other children recite by the hearth.

Limestone chimney is a lonely sentinel
over the long memories of three generations,
their voices silenced now
under stones too worn to read.

K. B. Ballentine

September Song

Dragonflies circle the lake, cool clusters
of floating hearts, water lilies dancing the bank.
The sky wide and warm, brushed blue,
but gray edges the horizon,
a breeze wrinkling the surface.

September floats in on summer's last breath.
Air crisps, haze wanes, and traces of orange
and ochre tint the trees.
Moss kisses bark and stone
while clusters of dragonflies circle the lake.

Voices glide across the water, sails flap
as wind fills, furls then moves on.
Shouts and splashes infuse the heat.
Paddles anchored, canoes drift
the bank where floating hearts and water lilies dance.

Fishing poles, pails line the shore—
a sandal, towels stripe a shaded lawn.
Far off, a motor growls then fades
as noon lulls the lake,
sky wide and warm, brushed blue.

No rain all summer, blackberry brambles dry and curl,
grass fading, bleached by August sun.
Daisies droop, but black-eyed susans glow
in clumps of gold. Jasmine and honeysuckle fade
as gray edges the horizon.

Water laps the bank, wind pushing its way
into the day. Coconut, piña colada perfume
the coming twilight. Against the pinking horizon,
boats, floats pull ashore,
and an autumn breeze wrinkles lake's surface.

Coleman Barks

Hummingbird Sleep

A hummingbird sleeps among the wonders.
Close to dark, he settles on a roosting limb
and lowers his body temperature
to within a few degrees of the air's own.

As the bird descends into torpor,
he assumes his heroic sleep posture,
head back, tilted beak pointing to the sky,
angling steep, Quixotic, Crimean.

This noctivation, the ornithologist word for it,
is very like what bears do through the winter.
Hummingbirds live the deep drop every night.
You can yell in his face and shake the branch.

Nothing. Gone. Where? What does he dream of?
He dreams he is the great air itself, the substance
he swims in every day, and the rising light
coming back to be his astonishing body.

Got to Stop

This highlife has got to stop,
this looking up the roots of words in the dictionary,
like *lukewarm*. I'm serious.

This eating and drinking and walking around in the neighborhood.
Way up in the Himalayas there are ants, several distinct varieties,
little lines of them along the grey rocks.

How did they get there? They walked.
No. They existed. This existing has got to stop.

This assuming of an audience. This taking of medicines,
with music in the background,
"Dancing in the Moonlight,"
book open on the table again,
this time to *peregrine*.

Glad

In the glory of the gloaming-green soccer
field, her team, the Gladiators, is losing

ten to zip. She never loses interest in
the roughhouse one-on-one that comes

every half a minute. She sticks her leg
in danger and comes out the other side running.

Later a clump of opponents on the street is chant-
ing, WE WON, WE WON, WE . . . She stands up

on the convertible seat holding to the wind-
shield. WE LOST, WE LOST BIGTIME, TEN TO

NOTHING, WE LOST, WE LOST. Fist pumping
air. The other team quiet, abashed, chastened.

Good losers don't laugh last; they laugh
continuously, all the way home so glad.

Tina Barr

Hour of the Cardinals

A judge from Tupelo tells me tankers
piss dioxin past the shotgun shacks.
Done eat the asphalt white.
"Drive til it's empty" is what they told.

Sparrows come through portals
in the chain link windows. Colic
means *inconsolable*, my sister tells me.
The Pope knew about the gassing of the Jews.

He turned like an eggplant when he died,
all black. In my dining room, a horse
comes through the wall, pastels scratched
against the surface of white-washed feed sacks.

At five, in the winter, they come
six or seven, red-feathered in the boxwood,
for sunflower seeds, a heat's compression
soaked into the cobbled face of a flower.

Abuse travels inside like the shadow of a ricochet.
Lawanda left with her girlfriend
for one of the Carolinas. She emailed
to tell me she'd seen the sea.

Guns Not for Sale

In the pawn shop cases, gold bands are snuck
into black velvet slits. Little beds of loss,
seeded under Windexed glass, blue water
drops, a benediction. A sign reads *License
Being Renewed.* My first husband gave me
a forty-five, nickel-plated; I hit the target's
eye the first try. They carry scooters,
motorcycles, chainsaws. Mylar balloons
bounce like silver heads. The stiff-haired
blonde is cordial; she gets to wear the cocktail
rings. Her linoleum is buffed; in the shop
window pennants flicker their tongues.
Outside, the paint is chipped, exposed wood
warps the roof line; a brimming camellia
outsmarts the neighborhood. Each flower tells
its story, each bud an explosive promise set
in glossed leaves, open-palmed, pink badges,
flat-faced ladies, yellow tasseled, desire spent.

John Bensko

To Learn of Feathers

When I find in a field
the large, dark-barred and stiff
remainder of flight

hugging the ravine's red clay
as if swept there
not by sky but earth,

my own body feels taken
from what's solid
and walking the ground

and up in air
all the same. I'm pulled
into the round, firm spine

and the delicate fine-comb
extensions that express
the lift and turn and spread

even more than the mind
that pushes them there.
Separation. Drifting free.

The air. The ravine.
When from the tree's forked limb
a spotted other watches me

blank-eyed,
the dilemmas of the night
freckle to stars. Those of the day

sink into their dark.
A buzzard roost of a barn
with its dirt floor scattering

of golden hay and black flight
makes me wonder
what I'd rather not know.

I drift to myself
in feathers and more feathers,
the painted, peacock

wish, the tiny yellow, lost
among the grasses
except for its brightness.

In the evening, when light
falls, my own
high-tempered yet drooping self

needs a limb
and finds a pillow,
support against the sky.

A Broken Ode to Snow

A winter day cannot avoid its snow.
Can I accept that I do not belong to myself?

On the street at night a flurry of shadows falls
across the light. Can I think that I will not be?

My feet leave impressions
that the snow itself cannot remove.

Things melt. Hair grows gray, then white.
Disappearing, can I think those I love will be gone too?

I love snow, when it falls fast and thick,
when the wind takes it and throws it up against itself.

To explain me to me. To know
exactly what I am, and am not.

Snow does not worry, does not toil.
Its only order is to fall and deepen.

When we unbecome ourselves, when we melt
in moments we cannot bear, who do we become?

I like to watch the snow melting leave the footprints. The icy
remainders where I've gone down the walk are the last to go.

People like to speak of the soul, and the soul's awakening.
It drifts, it rises and falls, it deepens.

Watching at night, I wonder how thick it will be by morning.
In the day, I hope it won't stop before night.

Peter Bergquist

Roosevelt

One summer after freshman year
I got a job through my father
down in Memphis, Tennessee.

They made me carpenter's assistant
on a big construction site,
which was work I'd never done.

Another helper on the project,
a man called Roosevelt,
showed me how to do it
because they told him to.

He was black,
maybe fifty, a grandfather
with some kids in college.
He'd done it all his life,
learned every trick there was to know,
what wood when, what nail where.
Before they knew they needed it,
he'd fetch whatever
for the white boys on the beams.

He could have been a carpenter,
the best one of the bunch,
but they wouldn't let him in the local.

I've never met a man before or since
named for a President of these United States.

That's not why I remember him.
He sticks cause he was major league,
made to play the minors all his life,
but nonetheless a pro.

I left the South when summer ended
and, as luck would have it,
never lived down there again.

Diann Blakely

History

It's blood, and generals who were the cause,
Shadows we study for school. In Nashville, lines
Of a Civil War battle are marked, our heroes
The losers. Map clutched in one fist, my bike
Wobbling, I've traced assaults and retreats,
Horns blowing when I stopped. The South's hurried
And richer now; its ranch-house Taras display
Gilt-framed ancestors and silver hidden
When the Yankees came or bought at garage sales.
History is bunk. But who'd refute that woman
Last night, sashaying toward the bar's exit
In cowboy boots to drawl her proclamation?—
"You can write your own epitaph, baby,
I'm outta here—*comprendo?*—I'm history."

Hellhound on My Trail

As if snakes and mosquitoes weren't enough.
As if trees, flaming in late sun, weren't morgue
    And cradle both: *blues falling down*
    Like hail like hail. As if fanged howls

Weren't echoes on this summer's trail, littered
With skulls. And now cicadas, and the vomit
    Of my neighbor's Bichon Frise,
    Who eats them live or otherwise,

The males' wings calling, with loud-trembled chords—
Blues falling down like hail like hail—for brides
    In twilit veils, lethal and silent
    As a man driving, one hot night,

Up from Greenwood to "shoot himself a nigger."
Greenwood: that's where you died, years earlier.
    Each summer stinks of ones before.
    My neighbor, her cancer returned,

Sinks toward the porch. *You sprinkled hot foot powder*
All around my door All around my door
    And it fell silently as blood,
    As silently as dead cicadas

Or those just-hatched to dig through humid grass
And sleep for thirteen years. Each summer's slap
    Revives old echoes: ask shot Evers,
    Exhumed from mud three decades later;

Ask my neighbor, whose dog howls each hot dusk.
If today was Christmas Eve O if today was
    Christmas Eve, wouldn't we have a time?
    Is your true grave at Mt. Zion,

Where I fell on my knees, or in that field
Of Greenwood's poor? As if death comes for free,
    A one-night stand. For brides, a veil,
    For murderers, a dirt road's embrace,

For bluesmen, loud cicadas and *leaves tremblin'*
On the tree. As if love, like hate, weren't a sin
    Original as hell's hot birth:
    Each song consumes the singer's breath.

Leslie D. Bohn

The Herbwife

for Dorothy

The way a lover longing to
possess his paramour will
fall on her:
ax falls into wood.
Split, it opens slowly from the blade
and falls aside,
a piece to the left, a piece to the right.
Sweat gathers in
her weathered grasp.

She searches for pokeweed and mayapple.
Her daughters sneak blackberries into
the corners of their mouths until they find
sunning on a bed of silt in the stream
a cottonmouth.
"Fetch me a rock."
The girls grin with purple lips,
seeds stuck like ticks to their blood-red gums.
She smiles, could tuck him
in the hole in case her husband or the law looks
beneath the linoleum
where she keeps her strongest teas
and Nettle beers.
The girls bring a rock, wide and heavy.
Holding it with both hands, she crushes
the head like Eve would've done
had she her babies then to think about.

Shadows swoop over her
of clouds or birds
or maybe heaven's truant children
bringing the breeze between them—
white chain of horehound
to garland her neck and sinewy arms.

ಛ

She strips off beige stockings,
slips her spotted hand inside the wide mouth
of the Mason jar, cups brine of manroot,
then bathes her arthritic knees and gouty feet.
The phone rings. Reaching to answer,
she leans out of the lamp's shallow
pool of light. Night fills
the hollows of her face.

Gaylord Brewer

When I'm Gone

Front lights will still glow
across the porch I built, still fail
against the winter night.

Moon and stars still hang
sharply in determined positions
of gods and fortunes.

The dog, no longer young
but still painless in her joints,
will still sit attentively

on earth on a loose leash,
accustomed to the house
down the road no longer new,

flickering mirage
that once so disturbed her peace.
She'll be dreaming of someone

else, awaiting someone else,
as will my wife here or elsewhere.
This all as it should be.

More ornamental bones
in the frozen ground,
the world spinning toward
spring even as it seems so still.

Interruption: A Coyote in Tennessee

A scream began it. I was at the door
in seconds. Along perimeter of woods,
she limped our lawn as we gawked.
Small across brutal evening, coat
darkly silver. Doggedly to somewhere.
I'd sighted one in the drive a decade ago

through headlights and fog, a story
no one believed. What choice now?
I snagged binoculars and followed
down that same gravel path. Followed
across our mowed field, toward
the trafficked highway. For a moment lost

in wild fescue the county had let go,
she appeared, tentative at the edge
of pavement. A truck with black windows
had pulled aside twenty feet ahead,
waiting. As she peered across two lanes
toward what was there, I focused—

snout, taut ears, tail. Ashen fur.
Dark eyes. *If you're determined to cross,*
damn it, then cross. Cross now if you will.
The pick-up growled. I lowered the glasses.
With balletic grace, she crossed.
Crossed the white line, yellow, white.

Soundlessly crossed rippled heat,
beautiful, hopeless moment, limping
past the barber's trailer, sharply east
for denser woods. A black window lowered.
Its fleshy face stared at me. "Red fox?"
When my wife screamed, I had been

deviling eggs, thinking vaguely
of my tired life, its trite yearnings.
The human face called out again
as I backed away. The limp worried me,
as did the future, and I wondered
what accident or attack sent her running.

Bill Brown

My Mother's Soul

My mother looked like a soul
waiting to be surprised. Whether
stirring soup or weeding a garden,
she was fishing for the unexpected,
like the morning at Reelfoot Lake
when her pole bent double,
and she swung a large water snake
swimming the air like a Chinese dragon.
She wouldn't just cut the line
and *throw away a perfectly good hook*,
so I pinned the snake's head,
threaded the barb from its lip,
and released it writhing
and scarred into cypress grass.

My mother wore a slight smile
that posed a question few people
wanted asked, especially the preacher
at Bible study, my sister on the phone,
or my brother sneaking in late
on Saturday night. A soul is what
she looked like until she died,
but forever is a concept I'll leave
to holy men on street corners,
holding signs of coming doom.

Give me something concrete,
my mother might have said,
like a snake pumping a fishing line,
or an old woman sailing her death bed
toward the Rapture, her faith strong,
her face like a soul, the morphine "O"
of her mouth dark enough to swallow stars.

And

Friday, home from work, I flip on the war
and watch a group of marines help a family

bury their dead, and it seems that soldiers
called the car to stop with bull horns, but

was the driver deaf? No one knew, so the car
was destroyed, and the Shiah women

wail and wave their hands against losing
what they love, against the charred remains,

and the marines stare at their feet,
and one young man being interviewed can't

look at the camera, and the Imam proclaims
them martyrs, says that they are already

with God, and the sand and dirt pitch
from the shovels as holes deepen,

and the desert sun cannot prevent
the holes from filling up with shadows,

and the deeper, the darker they become
until the bodies are lowered and

the wailing and waving of hands
continue and one of the town fathers

lets the translator kiss him
on the customary cheek.

Long Division

Walking beside Sulfur Fork Creek
a great blue heron stalks the shadows,
the shapes of painted turtles rise,
and a queen snake suns on a rock.

I think of poor Adam and his job of naming.
Even in the Tennessee hills the task is endless.
What was Yahweh thinking?
Some of the names must have come easy—

swallowtail, luna moth, bluebird,
violet, hearts-a-busting. But every bacteria,
slime mold, lichen? Even the slider
slipping into the water keeps its promise

to thrive and multiply. In this magical world
of physics and chemistry—do the math—
divide backwards by any number
and never reach the zero in creation.

I would look up the exact scripture,
but my wife is using my Bible
to press wild flowers—columbine,
anemone, flame azalea, larkspur.

Kevin Brown

Dangling

I have become an orphan
to language: my father, a gerund,
walking away, always

leaving me, never
saying goodbye;
my mother, an infinitive, sought to split

her and me
with adverbs like *quickly*
and *immediately*,

to abandon me at doors
of others' dictionaries,

leaving me without a word
that would welcome me,
spent my life looking,
thumbing through pages

so thin I could almost find
their faces on the other side
of the words

I was worried
would describe my situation:

alone too little, *ennui* too
forced, too foreign,
leaving me with *lethargy*

or *loneliness*
or just *too little love*,
only able to say simple
sentences—

This is—

unable to weep or wonder why.

DeVan Burton

Visitation (Every Other Weekend)

My daughter often asks why she does not live with me.
While I fumble through my rehearsed response, she tells
me how her stepfather teaches my son how to change
the oil, talk politics, and whistle at the girls that pass by.
They were not given a vote in how their lives would proceed.
Neither were they there to stop their mother and me from
making angels in the Kentucky snow.
Yes, the child support is in the mail.
But I will miss parent-teacher night to attend an AA meeting.
Someday my daughter will not ask to live with me, and
it will break my heart.

Thomas Burton

Sorta Resartus

Time to zip the bag again,
Once more to suit up in blue for a friend
(Not a wedding or birth, though somewhat the same)—
How long before the last, I wonder?

The suit, right fit though somewhat frayed,
Is worth perhaps what has been paid
And has suited me quite well enough—
Perchance it'll last as long as need be.

Melissa Cannon

The Vigil

A woman slips her hands through shadow, folds
the darkness over like a thinning quilt
so fragile she's amazed its fabric holds
the weight of all the weary nights have spilt.
Again, that rattle at the vacant panes—
and even though she saw the storm-struck elm
uprooted, felled, some haunted thing remains
and taps out absence with one phantom limb.
Her husband's grief runs a fixed course: he says
he lets it go because they must go on;
but how can he measure her suspended days
who, during those long hours before dawn,
turns only to whispers in his dreams, instead
of ghostly crying from an empty bed.

Chris Cefalu

Memories of Roger

Roger and I
drove from
burger stand to fish market,
from midget lunchcarts
in vacant lots
to faded green backrooms
of sundry stores
reeking of poverty
and catfish

determined to show me
"real soul food"
Roger wheeled his
pickup from North Memphis
to Clarksdale
talking all the while
about the bluesmen he'd known
and the cotton he'd picked
as a youngster
and the women who
were always so much
trouble

in moist barbershop air
slicked with mid-August Lucky Tiger sweat
I listened to Wade Walton
wail on comb and razor
while discussing Howlin Wolf's
haircut preferences and
grits and slide guitar
and voodoo and sex
while Roger smiled proudly,
and nodded,
"that's right, that's right"
a constant refrain,
those affirmations
of minutia and memory,

two older darker men
trying to make clear to me
how the world once
was

and Early Wright
gifted me with stories and smiles
between spinning records
like a ghost haunting the airwaves
from impossibly distant
radio days

standing outside
Muddy's shack
at Stoval,
Roger sang in his
rich, weathered baritone,
while I squeaked along on harp,
and then we piled into
the truck and went to get
some fried shrimp
from a beautiful dark woman
with beads of sweat on her upper lip
who looked at me curiously,
this young white kid
with the big black man
and then shrugged, deciding
it didn't much matter
and that shrug
was everything I
miss about the South
and have never been
able to make clear
to my dear friends
who watch their
weight and their
vote and their
cholesterol
and their
expensive sun
setting like a jewel
over golden California
hills

Handy's Children

The old men
dance to
blues music
in the
park on Sunday
and nobody's
watching,
the park empty,
the newspapers
skipping lightly
over the
grass.

James E. Cherry

Democracy in Middle Age

The Democrats are in Denver to call up a Black
man for the presidency
of these United States.

Three days ago, my doctor admonished
that cholesterol of 217 was ill
advised for a 46-year-old

man 10 pounds overweight
and that I am overdue
for a prostate examination.

I'm headed to the kitchen
for beer and potato chips
when my sister calls

from Cincinnati, wants to know
if I felt the magic of the moment,
was I excited to be a part of such history.

Sis, I know the history
of these white folks with their Willie
Hortons, hanging chads, swift boats, and it's no

way in hell he'll get elected. I just hope
the guy can stay alive
long enough not to regret it.

She chides me for non-belief and hangs up.
I take my favorite seat, turn up the volume
and await the Senator from Illnois.

Tomorrow, I will phone my physician.

Catherine Pritchard Childress

Putting Up Corn

In August, he places a bushel bag at my feet,
bursting with pride at the sweet corn he brings
from the rusty bed of an old man's truck.
Three dollars a dozen will cost me
eight hours. Shucking, silking, washing, cutting,
cooking what could be bought
from the freezer section where I find
green beans our mothers would plant,
pick, cook and can, planning
for hard winter which might not come,
hungry children who would.

I peel back rough, green husks to reveal
so many teeth that need brushing, smiling
knowing smiles because he has delivered
my submission.

I strip silk with a small brush,
turning each ear over in my hand,
rosary said to the blessed mother
whose purity he thinks I lack.

Our Father who art in Heaven, I didn't do the dishes today,
Hail Mary, full of grace, I don't own an iron.
Glory be to the Father, I speak my mind.
Hail Holy Queen, I called for take out again.

I cut each kernel lose with a sharp blade.
Shave away what I believe, what he would change,
scrape the cob and my soul clean,
leaving nothing behind.

I place a dozen gallon bags at his feet,
bursting with my sweet-corn yield,
in a kitchen where I don't belong, planning
for hard winter which might not come,
hungry children who will.

Made as reparation for being
the woman I am, placed in a freezer
where each time a bag is removed
he will be reminded that once, in August,
I was the wife he wished for.

Kevin Marshall Chopson

Portraiture

Tobacco—tips down
in greying barns
as this Tennessee
backroad bends.

Tobacco—drying on
the scaffold wagons
under a fading
September sun.

Tobacco—packed there
at the edge of the field
beneath the shifting shadow
of boundary trees.

Cut, spiked, and hung.
Waiting in the coming dusk
for a pair of eyes, a hand,
to catch the light—

hazed and fractured,
split by yellowed veins
and the day's darkening
on these summer leaves.

Samuel Church

Gifts from Grandfather

The sliding of a Case knife over whetstone,
summers spent hauling black walnuts until
my hands ached, letting me taste a few
without her knowing. Buckets and buckets
full of our shared labor filled the kitchen.
Spiraled apple peels spoke like winding roads,
the scent of wood stain and sawdust escaped
through the crack of the garage door. Once coal
blackened hands now clean because supper is ready.
The tattered King James and your dog-eared notes,
tucked away, buried in a life spent asking,
where does the time go? You'd always say
I was too young to know that it disappears
along those damn winding roads.
Curling round.
Taking hold.

George David Clark

Matches

Red-faced, arguing briefly
their one point against the night,

or blackened, sober as blown
light bulbs, they are communicants

in the Eucharist of brilliance
and will not be ashamed.

Infernal dragonflies, their wings
torn off. Informal flames on crutches.

I use a fresh match like a needle
to sew a gown of blue fire

for my wife. I hold a spent match
like a pen, signing my name in soot

to petitions for firemen.
When the night holds me

by the shoulders how a deep chill
holds me, I open a matchbox

like a warm canteen and drink
deeply the fermented lumens.

Studying the Book of Matches,
a man goes blind. That testament,

which includes the diary
of an arsonist's daughter—

her virginity like a fistful of tinder—
is the history of glory

in the language of ash.
It will always be the hidden

tonnage of match-light that can truly
confound us, how the mutable

glister on the end of a splinter
might be the name of God.

Lullabye with Perigee

On the dock in muggy owl-light
they badger her ears: katydids, a mockingbird,
the tethered jon boat knocking and knocking.

While the lake rolls over, spoons the spillway
talking gibberish in its sleep, she is silent
how that cypress struck by lightning
last July is stripped and white and silent;
how the Jesus bug across a moon enormous—
subtle flex of waterskin at his every step—skits
in awful silence on the fluent noise.

She imagines every house on the lake
undressed of its siding, insulation, walls,
pictures the whole road's host of sleepers exposed
in simple house frames with the spondee of bullfrogs
confusing their dreams and fireflies
pulsing soundless alarms through the bedrooms.

Of the contracts she made young with this world,
all have been broken and broken. The light
like a thin sheen of ice on the grass.
Someone, by now, should have heard her.

Jim Clark

Miss Ida Belle McHenry Recollects for Sarah a Memory from the War

I remember the first time a circus
Ever came to town. It was during the war
In Europe, around Nineteen and Sixteen
Or so, I reckon. I wasn't much older
Than you. It was "Stark's World Famous Show."
Oh, I can see those blue and yellow posters
With the elephants and acrobats as clear
As if it were yesterday. Pa woke us up
Before sunrise one August morning and took
Us in the wagon out toward Peytonsburg.
It's only a few miles, but back then,
In a wagon, that was a big trip. Anyway,
We stopped by the roadside under some shade
Trees and ate our ham biscuits, all the while
Wondering what in the world we were doing
There. It was a foggy morning, and as quiet
As could be, like everything was wrapped
In cool cotton. Pretty soon, away off
In the distance, I heard something that sounded
Like troops marching, vibrating the ground.
I was afraid maybe the war had come
To Kentucky! But right then, up the road a piece,
We saw elephants coming toward us.
Like the fog itself was turning into
Giant gray animals! They almost seemed
To float, they moved so gracefully, swinging
Their trunks and flapping their delicate ears.
Such power, to be at the beck and call
Of a tiny man gripping a big stick.

The Bearded Lady, Calliope Bondurant Jones, Retired, Apprises Sarah of the Rest of the Story

A long time ago, right smack in the middle
Of World War I, there was a circus come
Through here called "Stark Brothers' World Famous Show."
Now, the Stark Brothers' Circus wasn't much,
Just a two-bit dog-and-pony show
To be honest, though they did have a sideshow
With "The Man Who Walks upon His Head," a class act
If there ever was one.

                              Anyway, Stark's
Elephant, Mary, was by far the best thing
They had goin' for 'em. "Five tons of pure talent,"
They said. She could play twenty-five tunes
On the musical horns without missing a note,
And she was legendary as the pitcher
For the circus baseball game, with a batting
Average of .400. And yes, she was
"The largest living land animal on earth."
Bigger, even, than old Barnum's Jumbo.

So, they were coming down from Peytonsburg
And stopped and set up just this side of the
Tennessee line, a few miles up that highway
There. Now Stark – he never had a brother,
He just liked the sound of "Stark Brothers" –
Was a cheap sonofabitch, and he hired
And fired people right and left, especially
"Elephant handlers," who were just bums and
Drifters with no experience at all. He hired
This drifter, Red Woolridge was his name,
And Woolridge did something to rile old Mary.
Nobody knows what it was, though some said
Later they found she had two abscessed teeth
That nobody had bothered to treat and the pain
May have been part of it. Well, Mary grabbed
Woolridge with her trunk and threw him against
A refreshment stand. That might've killed him,
I don't know. But then she went over and stomped
Him to a pulp. I know it's pretty gory,
But it never would've happened if Charlie Stark

Had taken care of his elephants, and hired
Trainers that knew what they were doin'.

                                        Despite
The fact that she was his cash cow, Stark knew
He couldn't keep an elephant with that kind
Of a reputation, so him and the townsfolk
Decided Mary had to go. Only they
Couldn't decide how. I mean, she was *huge*.
They tried the obvious . . . went and got
The biggest gun in town, from the blacksmith,
And shot her five times, but she didn't hardly
Seem to notice. Some said, "Electricity!"
"Fry her!" but all they could muster was
44,000 volts down at the railroad yard,
And that just made her dance around a little.
Some said, "Hook her up to two locomotives
"Goin' in opposite directions and pull
"Her apart!" Some said "Chain her to the track
And ram two locomotives into her."
Are you gettin' the picture here? This crowd
Of people torturing this poor old creature
With their awful hare-brained ideas, each one
Worse than the last? It's a damn ugly business,
And a blight on the history of this state.

Well, they finally decided to hang her,
With a chain and winch, from a derrick car.
2,500 people turned out to gawk,
And it rainin', too. That's a lot of people
For around here, even now. They got the chain
Around her neck and hoisted her up,
But the chain was too weak. It snapped, and Mary
Set down hard on the ground. People scattered
Every which way, scared that she'd trample
Them all. What they didn't know was that when
She fell, it broke her hip. They found that out later.
She wasn't goin' nowhere. She was just
Suffering, that's all. Well, they got a bigger
Chain on her and hoisted her up for thirty
Minutes this time while the good townsfolk
Had their fun. Then they threw her in a hole
They dug with a steam shovel and covered
Her up and that's the end of old Mary
And her story. Not too pretty, is it?
What's the matter? You look a little peaked.

The Land under the Lake

for my parents, on the occasion
of their 50ᵗʰ Wedding Anniversary

I think of Noah, his family spared,
Riding that bark of gopher wood above
The good lands of home, now submarine, paired
Beasts below waiting for news of the dove.

Less sublime than God's wondrous instruction,
The voice of the Washington bureaucrat
Told of the Dale Hollow Dam's construction—
Good farms, long held, flooded in nothing flat.

One summer on a houseboat we drifted
Over barns and churches, cornfields and cribs,
Swam down, down, to where gauzy light sifted
Like silt through some barn's or house's ribs.

Marriage is an ark, with children safe below,
And love is the land lying under the lake.
In the little drowned chapel years ago
My mother and father slice their wedding cake.

Michael Cody

The Veteran's Cemetery, Early November

Early November, when his autumn work was done,
he left us standing stupid and staring
at the bluebrown of the coming
Appalachian winter.

He left behind his shrinking garden, harvested,
his expanding lawn, mowed its final time.
He left behind the handy man
who could fix anything,

took leave of the newly retired postal worker,
who never went postal, and abandoned
his role as little patriarch,
begetter of two sons.

He abdicated head-of-household status in
the house that was never his, left the loved
wife of forty-two years and her
overbearing weakness—

much too much for the Appalachian country boy,
who left his hills to see the world from ship,
from plane, from love in Amsterdam,
and then came home to stay.

That night he shed this life like Wednesday's dirty clothes
and would have been surprised by all who braved
early snows to watch him lie down
in a proud soldier's grave.

Lisa Coffman

Closed Coal Town

The mouths of the closed mines at Coal Hill have grown over,
but dent the hill's shape, like a body under the sheets.
The strip mines on Big Brushy Mountain have come back green,
but even those who don't know the ridge line find their eyes drop to the cut-out place.

You were bread, or prayer–a heat. Your knees pressed open my knees,
a turn of your sleek head could drive me a quarter-turn into the earth.
Your heart tapped out to me its code of hollowness, descent,
and I lay under you my body of empty rooms.

I came a long way to find you, as though I brought news.
I didn't know what to say; I pressed my mouth to your mouth.
And sometimes you moved above me, light played along a wall,
and sometimes your voice was close, noise tamped by a coal roof.

The miners, backing out, hacked at ribs that held up the mine.
Now the living are no longer enough to care for the dead:
the stones of untended graves stand in sedge grass's red-gold shine
and here, and here, a black seam breaks through its garment of dust.

Cumberland Spring

1.

Nights, I sit up too late.
In the morning, with what relief
I begin at one window,
watching only the old apple tree,
the small distances of birds changing branches.

2.

Pony bones and jonquils in the yard,
vertebrae flared like the jonquils.
My peace is with these sunning bones.
It arrived, I never did get to it.
What was all that, beforehand, for?

Robert Cowser

Backtrailing

Without a marker
there is no point from which to begin
a walk across a once-familiar tract.

Therefore, let me go soon
to a corner post in a pasture,
once the back of a cotton field
where a syphilitic woman lived,
like a hermit, in a two-room shack
long since collapsed.

From the corner post, darkened by creosote,
I will cast myself out of the crowd,
a coward though,
knowing that, unlike the woman
they called Evvie,
I can return by choice
to the arms of the world.

I'll walk northeastward—
exposed to the late morning sun.
The sand at the fence row
will feel warm and moist
to the thin flesh
of my bare ankle,
and the designing lizard,
a six-lined racer,
will scurry at angles
before me down the draw
where the insistent stream rushed
after a storm the week before.

I sense Evvie's presence and hear
the muffled voices of the Lofton girls,
who with goose-necked hoes
once chopped the cotton stalks.

Thomas Crofts

In the Graveyard of the Insane, Athens, OH

No names here, nor any dates.
Rooted in the rough grass these stones
like stubby irregular teeth, exposed
on the windy hillside
      where we are rambling
Rex and Augie, Molly and I, on the grounds
of a long defunct asylum: a gothic revival edifice
reared in the golden age
of lunatic sequestration.

Instead of names and dates you find
deeply cut into the head of every stone
a 5-digit number, by which the surviving relation
was brought discreetly to the grave
of deaf-mute sibling, spastic son or daughter,
crazy-talking cousin, demented parent, half-wit charge
or whatsoever relation it was
who had so declined in that asylum.
So small observances were kept intact

until, in some generation, the 5-digit number was lost,
uncopied, the paper it was written on
forgotten,
turned to dust in desk or keepsake box—
and by that process one by one
each 5-digit number on each stone
is freed from its indenture.

But now in the little daylight remaining
my sons are clambering over and sitting on
the stubby stones, complaining bitterly
that is this the worst vacation ever.

Kate Daniels

The Diving Platform

Halfway across the lake's dark span
The diving platform glittered, somehow
Suspended on the surface of the water.
Somehow tethered. Somehow floating.

It looked like an ice cube, he thought,
In a giant's mug of poison broth.
It looked like a tablet of aspirin, as yet
Undissolved in a sick man's gut.

It looked like a sturdy crust of cooked onions
Carmelized on the cooling surface of a bowl
Of soup. And it looked like a scab,
A monstrous healing, overgrowing

A wound that should have been sutured
But was left, instead, to heal messily, all on its own.

Ϩ

If he started now, he could reach it
Before he had to dress for the ceremony.
Before he had to free the rented finery
From its cloudy shroud of plastic sheets and fit it
To his body, tightening the blood-hued
Cummerbund around his waist and clicking
Studs and cufflinks securely into place
At neck and wrists. Before he had to scrub

The unworn soles of the black dress shoes
To remove the words his brother had chalked—
HELP on left and ME on right—
So when he knelt beside her to receive
The blessing, no one would know
How he really felt.

Ϩ

For generations, her family had farmed
There, in the fields watered by the pond
The diving platform anchored in. And not one
Of those persevering men could say exactly how far down
It was, how many murky feet of water before he'd touch
The bottom.
                So when he saw her there
On the other side of the lake, dropping her towel,
And striding straight into the water, and shallow-
Diving in, and striking out for the platform
In the middle, he understood how it would be.
That he would swim out, too, and meet her
There, and they would sit together on the platform
Anchored in the deep, cold water for a while,
Just keeping company, drying in the sun.

Moving

Old walls are new to me. Someone else's
babies were carried up this cracked brick walk,
sung over the threshold, bedded down
in the tiny orange nursery that gives off
the kitchen or in the low-roofed room upstairs
where I hope to write. Not mine
who took their first steps elsewhere
and never had their portraits posed by the short
stone fence or plucked the blossoms
from the magnolia someone planted
far too near the dank north wall.
Someone else conceived her creatures
here and struggled with the washer
in the cold, dark basement. Ancient
fuses, busted lights. Other
infants haunted these nights.
Mine are quiet and sleep straight through,
uneasy in new arrangements of their furniture,
new odors, new echoes. New light on the walls.
New darkness in their hearts. And while
they sleep, I pace my newly purchased
halls choking in wallpaper I'd never choose,
dark paints that sink my spirits. Wrenched
out of context, no depth to new life
yet. On the patio, a pail is full of water
but it's frozen. My houseplants perished
on the journey here. And the first garment
I retrieve from the packed-up cartons
is a shirt with its pocket torn off, still
wearable, I guess, but capable of carrying
nothing. No money or photos, no map,
no scrap of paper with a telephone number
I need to remember. Not even a pen or a pencil
so I can write my way out of here as fast as possible.

Sheet: A Psychology

for William Christenberry

Some people have told me that this subject is not the proper concern of an artist or of art. On the contrary, I hold the position that there are times when an artist must examine and reveal such strange and secret brutality. It's my expression and I stand by it. W. C.

i.
Because that form
Is still powerful to me

I went into the landscape
Never did I dream

a wedge of white wings
rising into the herald
of a hunter's twenty-two
and falling, marked

If I could take that
Form—the pyramidal
Hooded head—and transpose
This feeling that I possess
About memory . . . Beautiful
The way it cracked

into a bed of snow
destroyed by blood

ii.
It was dark
And the street lights
Were on

Ed said, I'm Jewish
I'm not going inside

Old marble steps
To the second floor

Eyes glaring
Through the eyehole slits

I went out of the building
Just like that
The form entered me

A death of blizzard
A murder of white

How could I
As a human being
Let it go by?

iii.
more than a few held the heft
of pain in their own
hands and judged the weight
too much to bear

and so drove it
down the road
to the homes of people
different from themselves
who wore no sheets
and walked about naked
in their pain

If you thought of the picture
As a dream or an apparition

but someone ignited it
and—through a plate glass
window—hurled a sheet of
pain wrapped around
a rock the size of a melon,
a cocktail of fire, a can
of gas. Whatever it was
it splattered on the baby's
bed and sprawled upright
in a flaming sheet
of gorgeous light.

iv.
These were tortured and/or
Bound & some had hot wax
Poured over them.

v.
Time goes by.
He hefted himself
into the cab of the pickup,
arranging the fabric in
folds, lifting it delicately
above his ankles.
He drove away
laughing, one hand,
on the wheel, the other
scrabbling in the melting
ice of the styrofoam
cooler. *Nothing more*
Than a distant feeling. He wanted
one more beer. He opened
the window and hawked
a thin stream of blueblack
haw into the white dust
at the side of the road
and drove away from that ruined
image *that building on a back country*
road with no windows and no doors

vi
The places that still exist
Things that I grew up with
A memory house, a group of similar
Forms, covered in white wax
I can't explain why—stabbed,
And pinned and strapped up
To various and sundry things
The things I grew up with—what you see
Is what it is . . . An environment is
An environment—you have to
Walk into it—Black memory
Form, Memory form with Coffin,
Memory Form Dark Doorway,
I was always attracted to the warped
Shapes, the strange and secret brutality
Right at the heart of it—I've done
A lot of work there over the years . . .

Ryan Dixon

The Ghost of Anne Patton

Beyond the orchard the old house still sits,
As firm—as resolute—as the blue blood
That built it—sank its timbers in the clay
And set the apple saplings in their lines.

The trees like gray soldiers lean against the hills—
Like those gray soldiers who came passing through
Between the hill and highway in their day.

It is said she gave them refuge in the barn.
It is said she allowed them fruit from those trees;
A little warmth, and rest, and they moved on.

But now the fruit drops for no one—
Apple, Cedar, Ash, have mingled there
In the brotherhood of a healing republic,

And she—arthritic, withered gray as flint—
Moves in the careful spirals of her waning days
That swirl her ever backward; always sure
The floorboards creak from firm and fleshy weight—
Of husband, brother, friend—
Always following echoes down the darkling hall.

She barely watches from her waiting days
As the apples molder underneath the boughs.

Each year the apples weigh the branches down;
She waits for something solider than sound.

Ena Djordjevic

Unnamed Language

The sky changing color at night, something I notice
in Vinca, my body less than one short trail
from that eternal river. My mother once said
that when she met him, my father would swim across
from his country to hers, shaking his hair out when he reached her,
waiting by the river bank in Croatia.
There is some kind of violent purple in the distance
above centuries of trees. A wind carries the sound
of the dead language, exchanged by a couple
passing in the dark. Behind me, the house is full of relatives
I have met once, between us a faint path
of what should have happened, if.   Had I known
the words would want me back I would have learned
to read this language. Now, it raises eyebrows in the markets.
I say bread, and they shake their heads. I speak: tomorrow,
goodnight. Nothing. Gone. Coming back here
is like entering a house you know
through a basement window. Relearning speech,
I am waiting to see a path through trees
when I touch my grandmother's arm. Soft.
Blood, my mother once said, is the way
we recognize each other, we don't need to understand.
The river is not motionless, as it appears. The river
I am seeing is not the sky, the changing
of the light like a pendulum in one direction.
I am one short trail from the river.
One short trail from if.   If is the violent country
I am living in when I speak. The river can't cross,
bridge. The trees by the water, standing or uprooted,
are shadows sloping into the bank.

Heather Dobbins

Picking Up

after Lucille Clifton

Maybe I should not have bothered.
Taking over like everything else does, a vine
doesn't have to be taught to reach. There is no rake better
than our hands. Sedum and lantana tangle into foxglove.

The woman has been here before but cannot tell me what she knows.

Torn stems feel liquid like my own mess
of living. Sticky, maybe I should have let it alone.
All that was dead beneath the low green canopy.
Where is the somewhere else I'm supposed to be?

Tomorrow there'll be more leaves. I'll take my gloves off so I can feel what's left.

Her knees like toughened overalls: no wonder she's good enough.
A burnt ticket falls from a river birch—I lean and grab, missing
the whole. Maybe I should have waited for autumn,
never mind drought, summer now crackling under my skin.

Foolheart in West Tennessee

These headstones go mostly unanswered.
June's fields are brown, a leather abated
by heat. Above silk flowers and carved dates:
clouds like hair on a salon floor, dead.

A foolheart will not lie.

Skipping stones, the water doesn't respond.
Penny-wishes only green the copper.
A songbird never calls back.
Lovers' names in ink on a river bench:
jeans and rain abrade the heart, the joining *and*
between them. A love letter in pencil
was sent months ago,
unreadable in a few years.

It isn't true that silence is wisdom.

Lisa Dordal

Wedding

As if the past were present completely
in the laden air of that June day, molded
by the unyielding stone walls of the sanctuary,

I walked, as my mother had taught me,
down the aisle, my body
pressed into taut, pallid lace. Her own.

Even the tightly folded note my mother
slipped to my bridesmaid to tell her
she was holding her flowers wrong

was a summons from the past
to get things right. And the look
I gave my Maid of Honor, straight

into her eyes during the spoken vows,
was a calling forth, a calling out.
You don't have to do this, followed by:

But you do; all of us—grandmother,
mother, daughter—there in that moment
of keeping and quiet, quiet breaking.

And the Gospel—slinked in by the preacher—
an appeal to rightnesses of the past, above
the muted aching of our female bodies.

As I said "I do" with almost every cell
and, in the process, began to die
the long and tight-lipped death of my mother,

who taught me how.

Donna Doyle

Holler

Raised in a house without air conditioning,
come spring, indoors and outdoors collided.
Sound and scent sifted through window screens,
let in and out songs of nest-building birds, fresh
mown grass, simmering soup beans, record player
crooning lovelorn lyrics—hello and good-bye—
gravel crunch under Daddy's tires coming home.
Best part of the day when he traded work clothes
for blue jeans, unhung his neck from a slick-knotted tie.
His posture shifted from the desk to the dinner table,
where my eyes remained open during the brief blessing,
holding present the man who had been absent since dawn.
Even now, enclosed in my own gray office building,
out of nowhere honeysuckle prevails, cascades down
the ridge, an urgent waterfall calling, hollering me home.

Tanasie

Come summer, my education began. Volume after volume,
pebbled encyclopedia covers imprinted deep on my thighs.

Tennessee, nine letters that labored almost across the state,
risen from Tanasie, Cherokee village, land before memory,

stolen from school books and history lessons, surrendered
in skirmishes between revision and truth right as rain.

Outside, my brother and his friends played, battled and fell
from imaginary horses, resurrected themselves, rose again

and again to suffer relentless killing, and dying, the part
that never lasted for long. In bed at night, one word lived

from lost language, danced prayers on my tongue—*Tanasie*.
From my nightstand, arrowheads pierced my dreams, sacred

ground burrowed deep with lessons, my body unsettled
by all that settled, truths that would never again lie still.

John Duck

Mackerel Sky

A nest sat on the porch in the space between pale
Yellow columns and the roof and, though I never saw
The inhabitants, I still hear the small, stilted songs
That drove the cats to the windows each afternoon.
Had them scattering across the living room, jumping
Over arm-chairs, pressing their faces against the screen,
Tufts of hair like young sores pushed up into the light.
A day's dirt and the afternoon rubbed red into evening:
Mountains cratered with starlight, as in the Greek "krasis"
Or mixture, my loneliness on a nothing day sown
Into the mounds of cloud's tilled rows. Herringbone,
Some call it, a mackerel sky. A boy and his father will drive
Beneath it, where dozens of failed farms flood over the road
Though the towns have populations of thirteen or less and no one
Around to give direction. His father will talk of the price of pet food
In 1967, mornings at the lake listening to fish jump in the distance,
And how to determine where the drop-line is. The boy will lie later
In a hotel room, boil under the sheets, push his fingertips into the wide
Pads of his palms, trying to bring the skin up around the impressions.

Benjamin Dugger

Vigil

in memory of my father

Loud, then louder, moans the patient
lost in dark morphinic stupor
like a thousand sirens wailing,
shrieking madness in my head.

Heartbeats mark each passing minute;
midnight stroke draws ever closer.
Pupils fix on growing blackness—
timely comes our final hour.

Soft, then softer, just a whisper
sounds this voice once heard as thunder,
muted now to labored breathing,
soon to sound no breath at all.

Mouth falls open, heart stops beating;
life departs his shrunken body.
Now my wakeful watch is ended.
Death has called my father's name.

Deep inside this quiet setting
stillness gives a gift of focus
wrapped within my new awareness:
silence conquers every life.

Sue Weaver Dunlap

A Daughter's Homecoming

Say it right—*Appalachia.*
Appalachia—at the end
latch the door.

But you didn't, you know,
latch the door tight enough.
Ever so timid,
I have crept into these
mountains,
your birthplace,
never your home.

I snuggled in,
pulled the covers
over my body.
I breathed faint remains
of long ago smelted copper,
a ritual baptizing
in Tumbling Creek, then
climbed high
on the Big Frog.

I can reach forever
backward
forward.

You didn't tightly
latch the door,
Mother.
Now I am
Home.

Renee Emerson

We Left Behind

Our first teeth, calcium pebbles
in the who knows where
of a landfill. Maples we climbed
and the stony soil their roots
run through. Beale, Macon,
Ecology Loop. Speeding
tickets. Taurus on cinderblocks
on my parent's lawn. The Krogers.
Sweet tea and lemon. Fried chicken,
okra. Mothers-in-law. Reckons
and y'alls. Unused wedding
gifts: twelve pieces of china,
a wall clock with off-rhythm pendulum.
My boxes of second-hand
books. The dresser my father built
and I painted blue. Our black
cat who killed squirrels and birds,
the copperhead. Garden flowers drooped
like golden bells and sticker bushes
beneath each windowsill. An outdoor grill
ashy with coal. The push
lawnmower. A house near the river.
The cotton fields tilled
and phosphorous in blossom.
Minnows, bread crust, green waters.

Blas Falconer

Maybe I'm Not Here at All

Two cars crash, the drivers thrown to either side
of the road. They lie in the dark for hours

before anyone finds them. Until then,
all one has is the other and the occasion:

a cough of blood, a kind of drowning.
They will each other to live without a word.

When I was young, a bus ran into a tree,
and children flew for the first time,

their hands open and stretched in front of them.
Even the long seats, bolted down, tipped,

pinning one boy. One bled from his head, one
from her thigh. They pulled us out and set

us down in the field, the grass, cold and wet
on my back. My brother bent over me

to say, *If the engine blows . . .* , and rushed
into the woods. The maple's orange fringe,

its red heart. The shallow sky. Could this
be true? They sawed the driver's head free

from the wheel. I remember her brown curls.
I loved her. When I closed my eyes, I heard

a valve hiss, a whimper. You fall asleep, first.
You turn and stir. You breathe the heavy air.

The Annunciation

Whether she lifts a hand to her breast in protest or
surprise, I can't say, though we know how it ends.

He reaches out as if to keep her there, her fingers on
the open book of prayer or song, the cloth draped

across her waist. *Faith*, he might have said, even as
the cells of disbelief began to multiply: a son

who'd face great pain? Certain death? In one account,
she fled. He chased her back into the house—

not as Gabriel but a pull inside the ribs until
she acquiesced, exchanging one loss for another.

X-rays expose a sign of someone else's brush.
Experts doubt the dress or wings are his

but claim the sleeve, the buttoned cuff,
a triumph, young as the artist was, not having found

perspective: the vanishing point too high, one hand
too large, the flaw in her face: a lack of fear or awe.

Merrill Farnsworth

Storm Season

Hot meets cold
twisting the sky inside out
driving toward Memphis
your mind on the past
it's midnight in mid afternoon.
Fields on fire with lighting strikes
hail clattering on the windshield
any minute the rain will come
pouring down like Noah's flood
and us, like all the other sinners
racing for shelter, hearts beating fast,
wedged between a pair of big rigs
hovering like giant bugs.
A Wonderbread sign flies by
and we laugh.
you and me
rocked by the wind,
nowhere to go and nothing to do
but wait it out in this landscape
of delta blues.

William Robert Flowers

Showing You the Old House

As we walk by the garden that runs
the length of the western wall, I stoop
to pick a leaf from the sage bush
my father planted the year our family
moved to this house. I can still see
him, bruising the leaves to release
their perfume, rubbing the darkened
flesh on the back of his wrist. Now,
years later, I recall the simplicity
in his gestures, the delicacy of the leaves
in his hard hands. So I show you
the garden, marigolds glaring, sunflowers
warping beneath their own weight.
I show you the hummingbird vine
with its thin violet buds all wound
through the posts that support the deck,
climbing the iron lamppost and swinging
bell. The magnolia drops its burden
of petals onto the grass. It seems
the sun pours right through us.

In the Second Summer of the New Millennium

We found an old air pistol
on the top closet shelf, scraped
change for pellets and went on a rampage.
Soon, enough of the locust
swarm died that they began fleeing
before us, emitting strange insect
sirens of alarm to each other en masse.
It was our last summer to be children.
I was home from college, listless,
unemployed. Brennen lost his job
when he caught his mom screwing
his boss, so we stayed as stoned and drunk
as we could, having no money but all
day, every day to fill. It was terrible
not being anything yet, our whole environment
turned like a mirror on that selfsame emptiness.
I remember the locusts scattering
down the drive when we approached,
how pitiful they sounded, how numb
I felt, watching Brennen hold one by the wings
and rest the barrel against its head.
Again and again, the cruelties of children,
and that insect whine of helplessness.

Kitty Forbes

Soft like a Chainsaw

Your voice sounds like blue-tail flies
trapped against a pane
like someone saving sinners
like a breeze blowing in a gourd
like banjoes from hell
a runner-up in a hog-calling contest
five pounds of bacon being fried.

Like a stage full of local talent
like a fiddle playing sharp
like someone's long fingernails
scratching over an emery board
an egg-sucking dog
chewing on a chicken
grits hitting the fan.

Like someone stepping on a bullfrog
like a hundred boots scraping the mud off
like someone flicking a Bic in the back seat
a mosquito whining under the bill of your baseball cap
tobacco juice hitting a fly ball in mid-air.

Like the bus pulling out of Pulaski
like a waitress reciting the specials
to a table full of drunks
Like static on WSM radio
horns honking
knuckles cracking.

Like a squad of cheerleaders in cowboy boots
jumping up and down on cars in a parking-lot
Like a couple yelling in the next motel room
nine hounds howling
in the back of a pick-up—

Like the sound I heard while napping in the hammock
and someone walked across the porch jingling the keys to the Bronco.

Lucia Cordell Getsi

Inside the Light, the Figure that Holds Us

Monet's poplars slide through the bright surfaces of water
their slender wands; they rise through sky

the color of the water, opaque, substantial
enough to hold the V-curve of leaf canopy

that suggests perspective, flattened into painting
after painting, blurred to background or focussed,

distinct, as though by telephoto eye so mesmerized
by sun the shape has burned into the lens and left a scar

overlaid by a rhythmic imaging of light that hunts the soul
of the scar by reflection, the way the water reflects

the sky, the way the eye hardly notices
the blue-green smudges of bank where the image

reverses, sending the long stems like roots
into the viscous gelatin of retina; it requires

an edge, the edge a frame, that we may see inside
the curving billow of leaves the classic form, like a chevron

of geese going south or north with the alterations
of light, that has flown into the very window

of the eye, broken it a little in tiny cracks, so that the gaze
prefigures the repetitions, like a memory of home, a mirror.

Quartet

Just before she is	dissolved	to music	the angle of
a hand	to birdwing	fingerfeather	bows
a line	brown	that drowns	the shape
of throat	curve of bass	the hip arc	of arms
impossibly long	head rest	low throttle	hum
that soughs	at the breast	and knees	in sepia tones
like a history	that sings	through fasciae	sinews
of sound	the surface	petitioning	splintering
prisms	to reframe	the symmetry	the *legato*
mobile	electricity	of stained glass	sewn
into repetitions	of syntextual	fascicles	in reverse
of the universe	opera	of light	threading fractals
in self-simulacra	tensile textile	tethers	of vibration
repetitioning	the figure	the lone line	of melody
the harmony	rebound	in the harmonic	rebound

Ron Giles

Seining Six Mile Creek after an Argument

First tip the silver bucket, with its perforated inner pail,
        into the water at the creek's edge, letting it fill
to the brim. Leave your girlfriend on the bank; wade out

        in your hip boots where the flow dips and glides
around boulders. Set the bucket on table-stone downstream
        from minnows in a pool where gray mottled

bedrock declines against the underswirl. Ask her to take
        the fine, double scroll of netting, wrapped
tight on two wooden poles, and gently pay to you the end

        that, when gripped like handlebars, spins free
the seine even with your thumbs. Rolling out seven feet,
        back carefully into Six Mile, while she follows

barefoot in the shallows, holding the net tautly over water.
        Center on the minnows, bright as promises
unkept. Scoop under the frenzied school until her eyes

        level with yours. Let the minnows settle down
toward the middle, keeping them submerged, as you both
        furl the seine, like kneading dough, until you

rise close enough to kiss her. Then raise the upstream side
        of the seine until you can tilt the minnows
easily into the bucket. (If she does not want to wade

        with you, take your grandpa's old green glass
minnow trap, about the size of a gallon jug, with one side
        flat and a wire handle on the rounded side. Aim

the end with the inverted funnel upstream; then lounge
        beside her on a rock and wait five minutes.)
An easy drive from Six Mile takes you to the river lock

where, walking down to roaring tailwaters
of the dam with bait and tackle, you steady each other
with your free hands, all the while thinking

how you will say that *plenty ought to be enough* when,
immersing your hand in the shiny bucket,
to nab one of the teeming minnows, you come up empty,

fingers dripping water. Take her laughing
as a truce, and grabble once again. Seize a slippery one
to bait a hook for her, then for you. Fish.

The Way It Was Left

Against a barn, splashed by July's early
brushing sun, a sign, in yellow script, welcomed
Debby back from the sand, where living
meant that luck had left a trail to follow home:
to bluegrass, windless and biding time
in the meadow; the cows and goats, standing
dumbstruck in the dusty lot; a rooster
crestfallen for months on the fencerow draped
with limp catbrier, until nature roused
itself to Debby's disenchanting eyes. Kentucky
gulped and found itself unscathed: rain
falling by the church, its door ajar; the wrens
fidgeting about the eaves; buttercups
tipsy along the edge of the graveyard's gravel
road, and a beagle slurping a puddle—
all quickless, else back at Marrowbone she felt
the clover, squishy beneath her knees.

Lea Graham

Crush Starting with a Line by Jack Gilbert

Desire perishes because it tries to be love
& so, I think, why search or seek it? Entering
its way out the backdoor, calling as Narcissus
himself, curious to himself only—only

this echo. Yet, some days wild turkeys wing clumsy
across windshields, or poets come to town
& language flocks before flying south, before
jubilee, before hush & slack. In chance,

what we flush from beech & oak, or her flush blooming
at a table, remains, persists as flight, or flown:
trace of bird in my eye, balloon drift among sky,
proposing hand, arm. What is not sexual, though

sex is part, catches life *en theos*. Not love, but its
roaming kin & nonetheless, wonderful alone.

Crush on a Road Trip

The myth in America—things move:
Poverty lines & flamingos blush
to blackjacks & sumac, dashboard

hula girls mug at spinners, these night-
crawlers & minnows. *Mike + Lisa*
4Ever red on a water tower

adorn Friendship, Winslow, Welch or Asheville;
loblollies & felt-covered dogs bob *right*
on; peanut brittle & roadside zoos,

chicory & horseshoes voo-doo these chiggers.
There's sorghum for sale. Mad Dog & cullet
grade this road; pet rocks & mood rings mushroom

in Grape Crush, Red Man & Wing Dings—
whatever you might wish along
the Mississippi. Mules drown &

flogging spots spell romance in the voice
of Mr. Moon River *wherever you're going*
we're going your way. Go Fish across

vinyl seats. *Someone's in the kitchen with*
Dinah. Jimmy crack corn & I spy chrome
of a Nomad—or was that a Rambler?

Carol Grametbauer

Adult Education

Buy a reference book, something
all-purpose to help you distinguish
between flicker and sapsucker,
white morning glory and bindweed.
Study the photographs of mushrooms:
note that some, the blewits, waxy caps,
and russulas, have gills; others,
like the yellow slippery jacks, pores.
Search for the organ-piped coral
fungi, some white, some almost
pink; for clustered jack o' lantern
mushrooms that glow in the night.
Some quiet afternoon, lose
yourself paging through the section
on *Lepidoptera*—the tiny,
tailed hairstreaks, lime-green grandeur
of the luna moth, dream-world
caterpillars like patchwork quilts.
You can study on these things
for years, yet every answer births
a new question. Remind yourself
that life without mystery rings
hollow; that the most memorable,
most tantalizing discovery
always lies half-hidden
just around the bend ahead.

Jesse Graves

The Kingdom of the Dead

I have no crew nor fleet ship to carry me,
no ewe and sleek ram to offer for bloodfeast,
and do not seek counsel with kings and warriors,

only the humble dead, those well-known to me
and few others, who reach out in dreams,
who call back to me from wherever they dwell.

I would guide my uncle out of the shadows
to tell again of his pastoral boyhood,
running through fields of burley tobacco leaves.

My brother hangs back, still new to his ghost-life,
how to bring him forward, will he speak to me
about parting the veil between our worlds?

Not one ghost who greets Odysseus and drinks
from the blood of his flocks bears him happy news.
The lesson is long suffering, and why not?

As in life, so in the burdened House of Death,
even those who walked in glory suffer here.
I fear what I will see, yet still long to see.

Cinnamon

Some cool mornings, he nods again early
and coffee tops over the cup into his lap.
His fingers never straighten all the way out
as they once did, and their skin shines
like a waxed floor. He forgets to dread

the perilous trudge to the potting shed,
then to the goat's barn, the chicken pen,
and eventually cranking the truck
to drive with a silver bucket of sweet
corn and oats to the horse lot.

He forgets to hold his right wrist in place
with his left hand, and to clench teeth
tight enough to still his tremoring chin.
But he remembers always the quick-step,
bobbing head, and nickering at the gate

that greets him, the split macintosh
tucked sometimes in his jacket pocket,
and her name, same as her autumn coat,
Cinnamon, yes, Cinnamon, which he savors
even when his mouth won't pronounce it.

Connie Jordan Green

Saturday Matinee

Even in hard times Mother and Daddy
found fifteen cents for each of us
on Saturday afternoons—nine cents
for the movie, a nickel for Milk Duds
or popcorn or saved for afterwards,
a book of paperdolls at the dime store.

My sisters and I sat through shoot-outs
along dry gulches, stagecoaches
overtaken by men with bandanas
tied over their faces, horses
pounding up clouds of dust, our world
flickering pictures in black and white.

All evening Mother hummed
while cooking supper, Daddy patted
her bottom each time he passed near,
we three girls with our heads full
of afternoon movies—Paula Peril
tied to the railroad track, train
whistling around the bend, her fate
awaiting next Saturday, our lives roaring
down the tracks, obstacles unimagined,
Mother and Daddy still hand-in-hand.

Regret Comes to Tea, Spends the Night

She arrives as we set out cups and saucers,
fine porcelain from great-grandmother's
fiftieth wedding anniversary, says
she dropped off her half-sister Grief
at the house two doors down, needs
no invitation to come in, sit by the table,
peel off her gloves. She wears gray wool
too heavy for the season, dress that reaches
her ankles, exposes only her spiky
black heels, stiletto sharp
to pierce our hearts.

Pale Shadow

I pull weeds from bean rows while seeds
that spawned these stalks slumber
among a thousand kin. They will sprout,
the agriculture professor told me,

for eighty or ninety years yet, their lives
a Methuselah legend my back
will never conquer, like starlight long
dead still traveling its eleven-million miles

per minute, messages our minds will puzzle over
until our own cells and senses blur and dim.
Knees in the dirt, hands searching and tugging,
I bring a temporary order—the same blow

for orderliness I've struck these seventy
years—dishes washed and stacked on shelves,
dirt swept beyond the doorway, sheets
washed, sun-dried, tucked over mattresses—

as if the world wants to be made
perfect, as if the living must print
their pattern, cast a lengthening
shadow before the face of chaos.

Rasma Haidri

Lottery

Everything my mother needs can be found at Woodman's:
cigarettes, milk, unsalted rice cakes, and six black bottles of diet cola.
I want to buy a lottery ticket she adds, weaving stiff-kneed, half-blind,
to the far end of the store near the videos and packaged liquor.

Neither of us knows how to go about it. I fumble, rubbing in the dots
from numbers she has already scribbled on a large scrap of cardboard.
I look at her familiar cursive and wonder what they are, these numbers
that are not our ages, not our birthdays, not her wedding anniversary.

That's six and a half million a year for life! she says of the man who won
last winter, and I don't ask how one figured the years left in his life.
Nor do I ask if that money could buy back her teeth and eyes. Her strong bones
and lean flesh. Buy back the summers she played squirt guns with us and caught
fireflies we froze and sold to science for thirty cents a hundred. *No one has claimed it!*
she whispers, as if everything is still possible.

Patricia L. Hamilton

Divorce

Why, with a bitter wind
sweeping across the empty plain
of our frost-bleached lawn,
is the neighbors' ginger cat
curled up at the base
of the weathered wooden gate
the handyman left propped,
too heavy for its hinges,
against our backyard fence?
Perhaps the cat sees it
as an enchanted door
from a children's story,
he the lion-hearted guardian
whose reward will be
a glimpse back to summer
when it swings open:
the hypnotic flicker of koi
in the circle of water,
the rippling red flag
of a cardinal's wing,
himself stalking a furtive mole
as the two little girls
glide through the air,
shrieking in delight, the father
ministering to the grass,
blessing it with sprinkling.
Why else would the cat
huddle there with only
a thin gray fleece
of clouds for covering, unless
to escape the chillier regions
of the silent house
without having to comprehend
the emptiness of the driveway
where he used to lie
drowsing under the shelter
of the father's truck.

Day of the Dead

Wisps of fog cling like cobwebs to the pines.
She knew the change would come,
just not this quickly. From the window
she takes in the red gash of maple leaves,
the bare bones of the old oak,
feels everything drawing to an end:
no more bright, crisp-apple days,
caramel leaves spinning cartwheels,
starlings like a burst of buckshot
against a sky so blue it might crack.

Last night she dispensed gold-foiled candy
to the tame, beseeching ghosts at her door,
her patchy scalp covered with a witch's wig,
a rakish jack-o'-lantern at her feet
grinning dissolutely into the darkness.
Now she shuffles to the porch, stoops,
lugs the orange bulk back inside
to hunker on the kitchen counter,
round and harmless as a harvest moon.
Candle snuffed, it's just an empty shell.

She plucks spent blooms from a marigold,
thinking how she'll miss the yearly haunts
of little ghouls and goblins; glances at
the packet of letters exhumed from a trunk
in the attic. Once she reads those yellowed pages
a last time, she'll let them singe and curl in the fire.
Who is left to care? What archive serves the ordinary?
In the late afternoon she'll drive out to the cemetery
as if to dine with old friends planning a reunion,
her hostess gift an armful of late-blooming roses.

Jeff Hardin

On the Eve of a New Millennium

Drunk off his can and pissed at the ruse of another day,
back-ache a bum rap and woodpile shrunk to kindling,
the old man stood at the kitchen sink and stared out
at his neighbor's cow. *What a filthy beast*, he thought.
What a stinking, cud-chewing, gas-spewing waste of a field.
And then, because what else should happen on a day as dull
as this one, what better way to stun the silence out of all
it cannot say, he stumbled through the ashen rooms to find
his gun. The front room table spilled its stack of magazines
and pens. He was not a man who cared one whit for what
you might have thought of him. He spat cruel words and mocked
your God and cheered the buzzards dropped to feed on roadkill.
What was all this talk about a new millennium to him?
Weren't the evening and sun the same as always, and nowhere?
Even drunk, he didn't miss, and the cow tumbled down
dead-weight and draining blood, and the good earth shook
on its foundation, knocked off its axis for a visible second,
the good earth clutched at the blood, drug it down, down,
and the neighbor boys hid in the back of their closets.
Here was a stretch of road a man like him could tuck himself
back down and not have to answer to a soul, least of all
some dimwit codger whose cow would stare him straight in the eye.
And then what happened, you'd like to know, as if stories
have endings that conclude or explain, as if stories heal loss,
stop time, weep light, speak truth, change lives, dream souls.
He tumbled himself into his truck, took off toward town
slinging gravel and missing the ditch, his arm out the window
conducting last light on the maples and shagbark hickories,
damning them all to hell, even the burnt stalks of corn
and the useless rail fence and the pigs caked with mud
lost somewhere he was tired of looking, and those bible verses
learned fifty years ago of the good soil and the bad soil,
and it took just a mile before he saw a car coming, and aimed.

Immeasurable

Having read and loved a poem by Neruda,
　　　　good luck finding it again
in all those pages, book after book.

And a passage, stanza, or phrase?
　　　　Might as well reach inside a waterfall,
pull out a lily or lighthouse—

the words will have turned already
　　　　to enigma or shade of acacia trees,
an incoming wave on the sand.

And forget trying to place again a single word,
　　　　the one from which you felt a shiver.
It has pledged itself to silence, wind,

aroma of some yesterday only your bones can know.
　　　　You are now a servant of uncertainties.
Having known and moved among borders;

having sailed through open doors and solitudes
　　　　and danced upon pollen, your mouth
open, tasting a pulse on the air;

having touched surf and shawl and the rain
　　　　inside piano notes lingering all night,
now you know nothing, a child again

who picks up rocks, tosses them into a stream,
　　　　each disappearing for perhaps millennia
or never to be touched again, like a thought.

How Many Lives Do You Have?

a response to Eli's question

Aesop cannot find a moral to my life, while
Basho tucks me in his knapsack, strikes out on a journey.
Camus turns down the café lights and occupies himself.
Dostoyevsky whispers in my ear and, running, I can't hide.
Emerson, at my funeral, shows up to read my journals' genius thoughts.
Frost leaves me in the snow-filled woods then hides his path's escape.
Goethe blows upon the pile of ashes I've become to breed a fire.
Hopkins harrow-haunts my hopes, arrests my daily wrestlings.
Issa mourns the loss of time that holds us both within its care, though
Jeffers gives the world back to itself without my selfish taint.
Kabir's ecstatic that I've walked out back to toss the scraps that
Li Po scrambles from the woods to sniff and steal away.
Melville bellows, throws doubloons about my feet, to which
Neruda writes some skinny odes that reek of mist and sea wrack.
O'Connor plays a chess game with my soul, her story's only character.
Proust knows I love the wind to last for days across the window screen.
Quasimodo takes his half of a parabola while I tremble holding mine.
Rilke sends me stacks and stacks of letters, rose petals tucked inside.
Stafford knows my face and name, says give them both away.
Transtromer shadows me, sneaks up behind, whispers, "Guess who?"
Ungaretti sings the music of a single word until the singing, too, is sung.
Vallejo walks across the street to place a crumb inside my mouth.
Whitman nods to me, the two of us hid out beneath the silence of the stars.
Xenophanes says together we'll revise those other poets' blasphemies.
Yeats gets down a book whose fragrant pages drift inside my dreams.
Zagajewski convinces me that I'm Linnaeus and everything's misnamed.

Kay Heck

Awakening Day

Tender bare feet *tap, tap, tap*
hard earth, anxious and keen
for the plowing machine
springing along Watterson
all the way from Striggersville
to dead-end Bynum Street.
Humming earth-breaker for hire.
Excitement builds when at last
we glimpse bouncing blue metal
rusty but for silvery sharp blades.

Our hearts beat in time with its song
as slumbering soil wakes to
the piercing, deafening disc-call.
Hibernation at last ended,
we run to christen the earth.
Toes dig deep in sifted ground as
our sacred ceremony begins.

Brother buries brother beneath a moist,
cinnamon oasis in a contest of who can
pack the other in best, but no one
ever wins, for brothers burst forth
from earthen tombs like Easter Sunday,
shaking revived loam from lean bodies.

I lie long in this holy coolness,
gaze fixed on a sapphire blue sky where
clouds become imagination's eye.
I am buoyant yet rooted,
dirty yet baptized,
by resurrected soil.

Three seeds already planted
before Daddy begins the first row.

Jane Hicks

Ancestral Home

Henry Monteith 1733-1838

Blood and bone remember
surely as nerve and neuron.
Sharp, sweet spring wells,
eddies through generations.

Redbuds weeping thaw
for blood and bone born
too soon, lying cold.
Sharp, sweet spring a cradle.

Blood and bone left
at fierce Shiloh, heaped
in sharp, sweet, spring.
Ghost pain—memory calls.

Blood and bone remember
fire, earth, water.
Elemental reckoning—
the earth thunders.
Sharp, sweet spring eddies
through generations, streams
merge in churning unity—
one believer in blood and bone.

Ryman Auditorium, 1965

I pouted and whined the whole three hundred miles,
would have kicked and screamed, except a sound
spanking follow. While Ed Sullivan touted the Beatles,
Elvis swivelled across the silver screen, daddy savored
the High Lonesome on thick 78s and slow turning
albums. Bill Monroe, Jimmy Martin, droning banjos,
chirpy mandolins, crying fiddles drowned out
my Rolling Stones. Our family flew down Bloody 11-W
rain-slicked and glittery, toward Nashville to sit
on curved church benches high in the Confederate Gallery
where funeral home fans pumped frantic rhythms to G-runs,
arthritic elbows bumped smooth-skinned young,
Beatle bangs mixed with brush cuts, lost in acoustic paradise.
I fumed, muttered, and strained to sit still. Flatt and Scruggs
ripped a swift set, caught my ear, then called her out to play
what my heart and bones remembered, Elvis and Paul forgotten,
I gave into melody and line, riveted to that pew
while Maybelle whipped that guitar into submission.

Graham Hillard

Lizard

It was only a fence lizard, a brown, mottled thing
that sunned itself upon the walkway, unmoved

by the childish thrust of the broom handle
with which I meant to kill it, took practice swings

whose wild arcs betrayed their falseness.
I remember the piercing fear, how quickly curiosity

gave way to revulsion as I imagined—what
did I see there?—its body beneath me, its desperate biology

a puddled stain in which a truth lay
fermenting, dark as mold. Yes,

it meant something to destroy even this body,
and I stilled my hand and called

to my grandmother. Hardly unbending from her gardening,
she crushed it beneath her shoe.

What the Ground Gives

After the topsoil had gone, washed away
by a crisp autumn of rain, stones migrated

to the surface and sat like dead testaments
in the clay, their faces aching for the sun.

The smoothness of them—things from the earth
should be rough and unknowable—surprised me,

and I pried one loose, a massive rock, and held it
to my nose, inhaling . . . fire? root? wood-smoke?

Or winter, settling in the throat like pepper,
coarse on the tongue like sand. There is

the possibility, after all, that we are alone.
I will take what the ground gives.

Rick Hilles

Missoula Eclipse

*Believe the couple who have finished their picnic/and make wet love
in the grass . . . Believe in milestones, the day/you left home forever
and the cold open way/a world would not let you come in.*

*(Part of the inscription on Richard Hugo's headstone in Missoula, MT,
from his poem, "Glen Uig.")*

If I could live again as just one thing
it would be this early Autumn wind
as it cartwheels the rooftops and avenues
of the Pacific Northwest; the way the air
of orchards vaulted in the mind of Keats
as he brimmed over with his last Odes
dreaming of the mouths his final words
would touch and kiss through any darkness

like a shooting star; the way a starry-eyed
stranger once blew smoke into the night
before offering me her cigarette outside
the 92nd Street Y, where I'd just given
a reading, so that I didn't even notice
sad-faced Jim Wright in a patch of leaves.
And there we were again, Jim weeping
and breathless to tell me he'd stopped drinking

and was in love; and, in a voice reserved
for children (and the very lost) told me
he had cancer. I wish we had hightailed it
then into my dream of Rome, the dream
where we are laughing at our dumb luck
and near giddy as we exit the gilded portal
and enter a day too bright to see the Spanish steps,
where, for us, apparently, it is always noon;

I always wanted to take Jim to Rome—
to see the black ink of cuttlefish
and shadows blue the edges of his grin
even if we were just to stand penniless and eye
the sparkling wishes tossed into fountains,
one whose water surrounds a sculpted hull
of a boat that's lost its mast, held in a state
of perpetual sinking as Jim points to the flat

where John Keats died, his friend Severn
at his side, drawing him over and over—
even after his last torment; Jim tells me
about the dream he's having lately
in which Keats appears, practically
flying up and down the Spanish Steps
in inline blades; Jim wants so badly
to grab the frilly garment of the white-

shirted Romantic, who now is naked
to the waist and in black spandex,
in death forever beautiful and ridiculous,
but Jim's afraid to wake us from the dream.
Still, there's a melody under Keats' breath.
It might be from Handel's "Water Music"
or just the syncopated rhythms of the boat
we ride, Our Fountain of the Sinking Ship.

Oh, to be so close to the poet we love
who died at half our age not knowing
what he would become for so many of us,
understandably, makes us a little insane.
Jim asks if I know what it all means,
and then he's coming at me like Sonny Liston,
as if the only way affection can be shown
between men like us is with an open fist.

And, forgetting a moment that I am
not even the merest breeze in your living hair,
and that a boneyard in Missoula, Montana,
negates this vision, just now to my dead friend
I'm real as any man who's loved his life,
and, stunned by it, tries to face what he can't take,
when the trees of Rome rattle their silver leaves,
and Jim picks me up, like nothing, in his arms.

From *Three Words of a Magnetic Poetry Set Found Caked in Dirt
beneath James Merrill's Last Refrigerator*

* Crimson * Ring * Touch *

It's true, there is no substitute for touch,
for the kiss that sets a world in motion.
One caress is all it takes, watch any nurse
in a delivery ward, each warm fingerprint

is gift. Whole histories of the heart
could be devoted to what passes
in an instant, from the snow of old skin
tumbling like dazed moths in a blizzard

of sunlight to what turns crimson
when the lit red fuse passes from lip
to tongue in a kiss first registered
as shock then recognized, taken in—

inseen. As when your true love
says, "Your lips—a kissable music,"
before nodding off. Leaving your mouth,
that inflamed ripe monogram of O,

an unkissed wish, that tremor
in your bones, restored. The residue
of touch, the lipstick crimson rings—
a nutrient set spreading in an instant.

Or at the promise of the touch to come,
a single note struck in the choir of itself,
when made to sing in us, is madrigal—
a resonance of every clear perception

of the world, even disappointment,
which might otherwise make for
a language cacophonous. But when
such sound takes residence in us,

the resonance instead becomes the love
we can do least without, the color of
a tapped black note, a surface shaped in
pressure—fissure, fault—of pigment, ink—

a single stroke, hoisted in the rafters of the mind;
which is just another way to know the origin
of touch as curative. (Being a little "touched"
is unavoidable.) But like a constellation

reflected perfectly then blurred in a wading pool
stirred by hand, the silver rings turn crimson
in a heart exposed, as if by touch alone, one
person, one life, might set a world in motion.

Larry Levis in Provincetown

(June, 2007)

This is how I am summoned from nothingness:
in faded cut offs, moonlighting at Connie's Bakery

where I keep reading Rilke to Jenny, the pastry chef,
who rolls her eyes & blows flour into my tired face.

Beneath my limp baker's hat & stained white smock
I still wear my favorite Hawaiian shirt, the color

of bubble gum, absinthe & night. We are permitted
to choose but one companion for the great journey,

so Garcia Lorca is here with me—we arrived last week
as "guest worker summer help." You'll be happy

to know that our work continues, as before, in Death.
Last night we finally had that conversation about

the moon & mirrors—why they can't tell us
everything they see. We stood at an ivy-lined gate

two summers too late to deliver Stanley Kunitz our best
vermouth & news of Roethke & the other immortal poets

whose ranks by now, at long last, he's joined. Instead,
our poet of black notes took off his white tuxedo shirt

&, facing Stanley's last masterpiece, his front yard

garden, which still revises itself in preparation

for his return, Garcia Lorca revealed thumb-sized
lavender crescent moons, the eerie constellation

across his chest above the heart, the scars of bullet holes
from Franco's *Guardia Civil*; he told me everything—

from the faces of the firing squad to digging his own grave.
He says the landscape of his dreams has already drifted

from the Alhambra's gardens, wading pools, & almond groves
to the salt marsh at Black Fish Creek & the starlit wisteria

he affectionately calls, "These endlessly creeping vines
of strumpet braids!" And the delicate braids of Challah

we braid each day rise like old lovers awakening to our touch
restored. You should see the lean, aristocratic

hands of Garcia Lorca—they've never been so strong!
I didn't think such mortal progress was still possible for us.

Or that I would again be permitted access to the knowledge
that comes in a love amplified by the stirrings of the world.

And then I recognized something in the insistent, winding
taproot of an oak, which pierced me with the recognition

that is holy, & I felt the tug of gravity's widening spell.
So that even if Garcia Lorca & I are just scraping by

with all the others working for peanuts in high season,
to be alive again & living in a hot seaside town

is good as any afterlife
& probably our best chance at happiness.

Angie Hogan

Apologia at Clinchfield Yards

If I rage like a circus elephant uprooting
turnips, trample pole beans at every turn,
then I must rage. Fuel for the fury
to try and stop me. Let me rage against
everything standing like an elephant
between us. I would have raged
past the tent and the river too, tossed
the trainer and his stupid stick aside.

If I have raged in circles, forgive me,
but let them be lariats of fire. Let me
drag them through the grasses all aflame.
It seems if I had raged brighter, we might
have taken the whole railroad down.

Lodge No. 422, Bulls Gap, TN

Reader, beware:
I cannot tell you the whole story.

I was standing in front of my mirror
in a felted blue wool hat.
Or a purple one.
I had nothing on
but a man's gray t-shirt
and thick boot socks.
I was practicing plies:
the eyes follow the hands
which move from front to side
to crotch and glide up
and out again. N the shirt said.
N for nakedness, nothingness,
N for his dime-shaped navel, his neck.

33 crows trample the bluish
sky over and over.
Signal light glares
with its one red eye.
I arch against wrung sheets,
hair dripping into the skin's hollows.
Bloodshot silk rises from the bedroom
basket, my robe levitating,
crows lifting it, half m's
at every stitch.

His eyes were bluish, trampled,
restless and reddening.
My hat was purple.
I called myself
Anastassia, Binoche.

Thomas Alan Holmes

Jones Valley

There was a walnut here;
wind broke it. A cedar thrives
now, offering meager shade
for survivors too past loss
to grieve. We count uncles
and aunts, those here, most at rest,
we stay long enough to watch
your cousins roll up plastic
rugs from around the grave's mouth.
You pull a rose from a spray
and toss it onto her casket.

From this hillside we see fields
fallow for years, overgrown,
pastures forced empty by drought,
winter feed costs, corporate
farms unable to recognize
any livestock dignity
respected by real farmers
who know a beast's potential
unpredictability
and stand wary, set to jump
out of the way, quick to grab
a blunt horn or a harness
or to strike hard and stand firm.

My family farmed here,
left here for Indiana,
returned here just as broke,
homesick, sick of Yankees,
sick of mockery from those
only a generation
more assimilated.

It was better to walk past
old home places lost to us,
unmade crops, mortgages,
so many sons gone to war,
still up north, not coming back,
having children who mock us
for being backward, Southern,

country, when we are cautious,
rooted, country without sneer,
without derision or shame.

I would like to go back
and give your newlywed
parents that hundred dollars
that would have saved that pasture.

I would like to join those men
waiting in the backhoe's shadow.
I can hear their radio
turned down in respect, of course,
but hinting of tackles
and first downs.

                    I would like
to drive you to that spring
on our old home place, and squeeze
green peppermint leaves and drink
ice-cold water until my jaws
ache as we ache as my heart aches.

Mandolin

> "Away with the noise of your songs!
> I will not listen to the music of your harps."–Amos 5:23

Too big a man to hold
a plaything, husband, set
it down, your mandolin.

There lie no mines for miles
around. You've always farmed
or found some joinery.

There's no black lung, no shafts
like graves; we've sun and rain,
a roof for night's relief.

God would not hear from strings—
the Scripture tells us so,
no hymns from mandolins,

such meager instruments
for praising Him. The Lord
told Amos set them down.

No lover lost, no one
forsaking you, no pain
from broken hearts, none gone,

we have our lives. To hold
a baby, husband, think
of it, to have a son.

To ramble on the road
is daydream, husband, meant
for boys who have no home.

To sing of taking off
and straying from your roots
might count among your sins.

We have a life to piece
together, husband. Set
it down, your mandolin.

Scott Holstad

5th Avenue Motel

They closed the transient
5th Avenue Motel and now
where will they go?
The single mother with
her two daughters
eating cockroaches from
the floor, hell, where will
the rats and roaches go?
The city thinks it's
a drug-infested blight,
but Jack Neeley knows
its secret history, likely
once a grand building
near Knoxville's 4th
and Gill district.
They came from all
over to stay for a
night or a month
or whatever they
can afford, however
they can afford it—
recycling bottles,
turning tricks,
playing at Robin Hood
for themselves, and now
it's gone, broken windows
boarded up, chain link
fence surrounding it
like it's a dog with scurvy.
The transient hotel
drained pale, pissing
into an empty ashtray.

Heather M. Hoover

Tigers in Red Weather

Lightning bugs flash in manicured lawns,
trains rumble past in all hours

But just beyond rises the tortured spine
of ancient mountains,
the place in my dreams, that I see
when I speak its name,

where laurel thicket tangles
with waxy rhododendron, smelling of green
and dappled light:

The wisdom of waterfall as lichen
munches limestone
or in a chorus of wakerobin
gathered on the forest floor.

And if I climb high enough,
I can still see the shopping malls and subdivisions.

But they could be anywhere.
And I am here.

Janice Hornburg

My Father's Room

My father's bedroom—
the threadbare headrest
of his rump-sprung easy chair
bears a concavity
shaped by his head.

His bed is neatly made.
Lined up on double dresser:
wallet and keys, a comb
with curly gray hairs
twining between broken teeth.

Cast-off earthly treasures
inside a jewelry box:
gold cuff links, an old wristwatch
that suddenly stopped ticking;
he never got it fixed.

Stained gauze and wrappings
litter the hardwood floor—
clutter left by medics
who arrived too late
to start his heart again.

His familiar smell
lingers on well-worn suit
hanging in the closet—
a chrysalis left behind
when he took flight.

Elizabeth Howard

Willow Withe

Grandfather humped across the field,
a willow wand grasped in his hands,
me a tyke at his heels.
Willow Withe, Willow Withe,
he chanted, lead us to water.
The wand bent to the spring's surge,
and Grandfather whooped.
Water, water, a sea of water,
come seabirds, run along this shore.
Grassheads brushed his trousers,
scratched my skinny legs.
Grandfather, longing for the old country,
ever talking of seabirds and seashores.

Early morning, I follow the limber wand,
as Grandfather taught.
Only the wand knows the way.
Johnny gone to war,
Grandfather resting on the hill,
I have to follow the willow.
A well, Johnny wrote, if we had a well.
I dream of a house
the way Grandfather dreamed of seashores,
a field where grassheads brush my legs.

The wand, like the snake
in the bird's nest, comes to life.
It bends in my hands,
dips, pulls, a thirsty magnet.
Water, water, a sea of water,
I hear Grandfather whoop.
A flock of killdeer flies over, calling.
Plovers. Seabirds in a sea of grass.
The old country come home.

Dory Hudspeth

Seeking Advice

Of course, it looks easy to the person
who invented the damn thing.
That's the last person to counsel which tab
goes to which slot, or which bolt to which flange.
I need instructions from someone,
with no particularly special insight,
fumbling to put the widget together—
someone who will plug it in
and stand back in fear of spark or collapse.

Despite good intentions, a bewildered new-comer
gives better road directions than the long-term resident,
who may have forgotten the street was made one-way,
or the landmark barn burned down last year.
I look for someone who was recently lost to lead me
through a strange town, someone who knows
what the wrong way feels like,
how easy it is to go astray.

On the path toward wisdom
the brilliant or saintly can't help my trudge.
I avoid exceptional people. I want someone
moving, but sweating under the weight
of a single grain of light.

H. K. Hummel

Tornado Season

The trunks of the dogwood
torque into a rip current of white petals.

Sirens descry the inrushing, invisible storm.
In bed, you make

your arms into basilica staves
and pray the roof into place.

Power lines lash fire. Neighborhoods
rupture into shards and splinters.

Some things we know
by the debris they drag.

The matter we learn
by what we try to hold in place:

this one with a body of songbird and timber,
a tracery of leaves and water.

Let the jars of sun tea, flowerpots
and trucks disappear up.

We have arms to asylum,
hands to minister.

Ordain yourself
and exorcise the sky.

Then bow into the headwind
as you must. Brace

until the house lands
and your lot is made clear.

When the mockingbird begins
she calls out for all of us.

Jannette Hypes

Blue Ridge Directional

for Jessica

To get here from your mesa, travel east until all you witness
swells green, your eyes wet like grass. Reach Gatlinburg:
slip half-dressed into the stream below the Chimneys.

Watch you don't dissolve: skin white as sand shines.
Hair darkens in the current to the color of poplar-root.
Breathe in the stony mist, submerge, bring bottom-rocks

up in the bowl of your hands. Call them Earth's bones.
Tongue and tumble each smooth stone to loosen, taste
what's not dragged downstream. Pray with whippoorwills

who gather among the rocks. Ask the water if what's swallowed
can be sacred. Carve the answer on glass, travel home to bury it,
one hand caressing the small mountain of zinc in your belly.

Richard Jackson

While You Were Away

Sleeves of sunset hung empty over the brown hills.
Ice from the North Pole kept floating this way. Locusts
sprouted like seedlings. I was floating under the ice
in my dream, but you never saw me. The windows were
boarded up. Later the clouds argued, then left in a huff.
There's a hidden tax in everything we say. I meant
for this poem to glow in the dark like one of those
old statues of saints. My father kept one on the dashboard
to guide the way. But aren't we always lost? Desire
punches a time clock that always reads the same hour.
There's a suspicion that today is really yesterday.
That crickets dream about being reincarnated as pure
sound. The bees wake as the sun hits the hive.
The sky is filled with late and clumsy birds.
Somebody's always ready to pickpocket the past.
There's a gap in the narrative the way a river
suddenly slips underground but flows on unnoticed.
Now they think the vegetative state has some neuron
activity. I worry that most of my own memories are
water soluble. There are places inside me so remote
the inhabitants never see each other. The worm never
sees the robin. White tipped reef sharks catch a prey
by sensing the electric impulses in its muscles. Auto-
cannibalism occurs when the Hutu militia of east Congo
make their captives eat their own flesh. Feel free to add
whatever you want there, but it won't make it any better.
Every war is reincarnated as another war. Even Paul
retreated to a cave in the Taursus foothills when things
went bad. He preached about love, but nobody has
ever really withstood its test. Some of his flock never
returned. *A species stands beyond*, wrote Dickinson.
Almost every species of small bird comes to my feeder.
Maybe everything is a test. Like how I am going to get you
back into this poem. *I'll git you in my dreams*, Leadbelly
sang to Irene. This was going to be a Valentine poem
because today is Valentine's Day, which replaced Lupercalia,
the Roman fertility feast, but that was before the daily news

broke in. And before tomorrow had already forgotten us.
The great love poet, Leopardi, never knew a woman.
Modigliani loved every woman he met and painted them
in order to leave them. Queen Nefertiti's eye make-up
stopped infections, but its lead base drove her mad.
She wanted to be born again as the brightest star. She read
her future in the cloudy hatchery of the Milky Way.
If space weren't a vacuum we couldn't bear its decibel level.
The Hutu slaughter women who learn to read, and joke that
it's a form of reincarnation. They think they live on
the dark side of the moon. The sky is gnarled with clouds.
There's a low fog covering another war in the foothills.
The stars are no longer the gods we took them for.
The moon is a turtle that needs to right itself.
I don't really know how to tell you all this. It's as if
I were left at the doorway of one of your dreams.
If only these words wouldn't conspire against me.
But even Love is an unsolvable equation. Leadbelly
kept singing because his own song never worked except
in his dreams. I'm still floating in mine. I don't have
any faith in a solution. You can't just turn off the news.
It's getting late—best to guess *None of the Above.*
All we have left is the astronomy of Hope. The hills have
their own geometry. Paul said we devour our own souls.
Maybe it's just the way the day grows up and leave us.
It all comes down to the same thing in the end, which is
what everything has been pointing to since the beginning.
When you're gone, you see, all these worries spin around
like those childhood tops that zig zag until they bump
into something that stops them, like this, for example,
another simple mention of you, if only for later reference.

Signs and Wonders

The morning avoids us. The streets walk through town and
never look back. Trees whisper secrets, and we think it is
just the wind. The echo of the moon is fading. There's a worn
saxophone in the corner filled with unplayed notes. The pigeons
on the walk nod their heads and mumble to its music. The water
a cactus holds is the desert music Williams so loved. The foreign
planet that has wandered into our own galaxy, origin unknown,
has a plan for us it won't reveal. And why should it? The soot
we leave on Tibetan glaciers melts them. Diseases creep
towards the warmer north. Someone invades a home or
a country, and it hardly wakes an image. A child is torn by
an abuser, and no one reports it. The man selling pretzels,
the man sleeping under the cardboard on the bench,
each one has his own shoebox of memories. Our own shoes
are filling with borders. The bonfires of our souls fall in on
themselves. It's as if we must tune our silences to a lost key.
Love? How do we give ourselves to another and not lose
our selves? We have to learn how even the objects around us
hide their pain. We can't listen to the heart's ventriloquists.
It's a fact that music raises our endorphin levels, which kills pain.
Ben Webster *In The Wee Small Hours of The Morning* would
let his tremulous breath slide emotionally beneath his
saxophone's sensuous fingering, but was called *Brute* for the pain
he'd inflict, later, in a bar. My father, listening to Gene Krupa's
wild drum, would say the emptiness behind each note is just
the ghost of what we could do to each other. How lucky we are,
he'd say, not to calculate the decay of our own sun. The light hides
now behind skirts of rain. When scientists let hydrogen antimatter
collide with matter, we delight in its pure energy and try
to ignore the destruction that always follows. These are all
the signs I know. They point to a world behind this one. Webster's
bulging eyes would tell us there is always more. The tracks of
the past outdistance our dreams of it. And what was he gesturing
towards, years later, my father, his mind nearly porous, seeing those
three frightened pigeons, if not the pure, inescapable flight of his heart?

Visionary

I could feel a few dying stars hovering over my shoulder,
but that wasn't it. Not the fact that there are so few
sunspots anymore and therefore fewer Northern Lights.
Not the problem of the thinning arctic ice. And yet weren't they
all connected somehow? Weren't they symptoms of something
I couldn't see. How many people saw the naked man fleeing
Christ's betrayal in Gethsemene? Fish nibble at the moon's
reflection. Camels have two eyelids, one transparent,
so they can see in sandstorms. We see only what we want
to see, only a fraction of what this stone has seen in a few
billion years. Now the stone wants to be an apple. The night
splinters. The sky trembles piteously. The real world appears
in the reflection of the soldier's face on a green radar screen.
Maybe there are some things we are not supposed to see.
The town beneath the lake. The cells that will divide mercilessly
in a few decades. I have been looking at Chagall for whom
every object is transparent. He thought that some of his dreams
were dreamt in other people's minds. That's why his images
echo each other from distant points on the canvas. Everything
we see hides a world someone else sees. If you don't finish this
poem it won't exist. Neither will I. Where do we come from when
we come to ourselves? There's a common thread that hasn't
been established yet. Cendrars said that Chagall, painted a church
with a church, a cow with a cow. He painted his own love, Bella,
floating up to kiss him. A hawk's flight unravels the thread we never
knew was there. There's a smell of smoke smudging through
the trees, but no fire. These words migrate towards invisible
meanings. It would be hard to predict what follows.
Each hour seems ready to kidnap the next for ransom.
How many orphans blindly follow some warlord around
the streets of Mogadishu with an AK-47 and sack of grenades?
This is not the symbol or allegory you might take it for.
Behind them, if you look carefully, there's a mother fleeing
her burning house with a wheelbarrow full of children.
She seems to gaze from the beginning of time. The day turns
into ash. The evening is exhausted. It lies like a shed snakeskin.
It is only slowly now that the poem gathers itself around
these unexpected events. In Chagall's *Poet Reclining*
the pastoral world behind him is both dreamt and real.

He seems to lie in front of, not in the picture. You can't see

who is in the building or in the woods. You have to look for
what is out of place. We need, like Blake, to look through
and not with the eye. The paths from here spread out like
cracks in ice. The skaters trace patterns you can only see
from above. How am I going to see my way clear of all this?
Everything I say brings its endless army of associations.
In another poem the woman would be pushing a shopping cart.
We can hope for another scene to emerge out of the shadows.
There's nothing we can do about the guns or the warlords.
It will have to show a way that looks like truth, but
it will have to show it through these broken windows.
You have to see it to believe it, but you'll never see it coming.

Mark Jarman

Fates at Baptist Hospital

A Godly life would be the best,
If it could be lived, so would Eden,
If we had stayed there.
Meanwhile we can choose a Godly life.

For Eden is still burning,
And the air scorches our lungs,
Our tongues, our young, and yet,
Another Eden remains a possibility.

To live for others,
To pray without pause,
To dedicate the waking hours
To heaven . . .

So I was thinking after my doctor's visit
And the tests and the reassuring conversation
In his office and the making
Of another appointment.

On the hospital elevator three women joined me,
Laughing, as one, the pretty one, sneezed,
The loudest, pumpkin plump with moles,
Cackled and teased her, and one,

A tattered coat upon a stick, said, "Y'all cut it out!"—
Conspiratorial, with no idea
That I sensed who they were,
Nor interest in me.

And I was thinking about the Godly life,
And how eternity might feel,
And yet, in their company,
Knew I was happy.

I found my car in the garage below
An image of a bunch of grapes—no letter,
No number—and felt lucky then
To be still in one piece.

That Teenager Who Prowled Old Books

That teenager who prowled old books to find
Any argument with a whiff of the Holy Ghost—
I meet him again in his marginalia,
Which ignored the common sweat and stink and marked
Those passages that confirmed what he was hunting.
There was the milk-white hart of evidence.
There was the hound of heaven, italicized bold,
Like an angry footnote chasing it off the page.
And there were the hunters, in pursuit themselves—
Plato, Lucretius, Virgil, Marcus Aurelius—
Who did not know he knew what they were after.
And so he missed a lot, all of it human,
Even while scribbling black and blue *Eurekas!*,
Bleeding through pages backwards, to note irrelevance.
It was all about something else, which he didn't see,
As philosophers mounted their lovers from behind
And felt their limbs go dead from the toes upward,
And poets kissed a mouth that fastened tight
And locked tongues and tried to catch their breath.

T. J. Jarrett

After Forty Days, Go Marry Again

Beslan School No. 1, September 1, 2004

She was only just here. That's her,
that's her in the red dress, that's
her, too, fists full of balloons as if
she would fly away. That's her at the
bottom of the hill. She ran as fast as she
could toward the top, arms wide,
cheeks flushed. She reached me
breathless and toppled both of us.
That's her, and her again,
her black hair in pigtails held
in yellow ball-stay barrettes.
Girls of that age are particular
about such things. I sleep in her room
some nights with all the lights on,
everything as she left it.

There she is in Rostov, there she is
and there she is and there she is.
There she is: bits of black hair
and the earrings. They say: *maybe*
that's not her. Look. There.
The ball-stay barrettes. Yellow,
flowers stretched around. There she
is at Christmas. There she is that
summer she grew three inches. They say:
after forty days, go marry again. But
there she is, and there she is again with
her friend from class. That girl is dead too.
There she is at the carnival. There she is.
Her fists clenched on the balloons. There
she is at the door, lunchbox in one hand,
waving with the other. At night,
I pretend to sleep; there she is
standing over me as if there are words
left to say. There she is. There
she is in the dark.

Don Johnson

The Importance of Visible Scars

(in memory of Leah B. Johnson)

Now barely scars, faint discolorations
summer sun darkens to stains
that trigger her one burning memory:

morning in her small first kitchen,
sun rakes the walls, and the room
would be breathless even in mid-December
from the steam the borrowed pressure cooker
spews. Big with her first child, she
thinks of its heart keeping time
with the steam's rhythmic hisses, chokes
off the rising urge to gag on air
too heavy with ripe apples.
Cortlands go bad in her pantry.
The peeled Delicious wait like small
white heads on her yellow table,

and something is wrong on this day
she would have sealed up in jars.
The willed heartbeat—No,
the steam has shut off,
backed up at the clogged valve,
ready to blow,
                blowing as her scream
bubbles out, heaving the sweet, scalding pulp
on her arms. Her baby's first solid food
is already slung round her kitchen.
It crawls like lava down her arms,
blisters her motherly skin
down through the third layer.

Now no one asks how the pale striations
she fingers in the warm sun came to be.
If he ever knew, the child, grown,
with his own family, has forgotten
how she carried him in arms swaddled

with gauze until the pain bled away
and she could touch him. She wants
to touch him now, to gather his children
in, tell them warmly that we all scar
deeply in that third layer.
But the words catch, back up.

The Russian Church at Ninilchik

Alaska, July 17, 2010

"Until they think warm days will never cease."
John Keats

The tilt on the graveyard's oldest cross
parallels the angle of the lowest rung
on the upright *Cruces Orthodoxae*
that surround it, the skewed crosspiece,
one end up, the other down, said to be
an emblem of the two thieves' fates on Christ's
either hand on Calvary. This leaner
testifies not so much to faith
but the ministry of wildflowers—
Arctic Lupine, Chiming Bells, Angelica—
that supports it, as the sanctuary's
new steel roof attests to glacial wind, sleet
off Mt. Redout straight north across Cook's Inlet,
lifting the metal panels, ever probing
the soffit's edge ten months of the year,
raising the question of why anyone
would build a church on this unprotected
promontory. The first thief's defiance
comes to mind. But on this windless July day
faith is effortless, when paradise seems
close at hand on this mountain of wildflowers
glorified by bees already tumbling drunk
by noon on the nectar of angelica.

Night Flight: West from Minneapolis

Independence Day, 2007

How clear this night. Twin Cities' houselights gleam
like soldered dots on a circuit board. Connecting
highways shine like silver wires that melt
as we ascend, and funnel to one unwavering line
of Interstate stretched to Anaconda and beyond.

Fireworks mark our path across Dakota.
Capillaries, red and orange, rise up from
nameless prairie towns, rupture, then flatten
without sound beneath the wing,
their radiation like night blooming cereus,
incendiary prayers that flame out
and fade, shock waves dissipating
miles below our cruising altitude.

And I ponder how the old gods, remote
and inaccessible, incapable of winding
the last threads of smoke from guilty goats
or smoldering thuribles, would separate
the blessed from the cursed. Or if,
weary of choosing, they yearned to come
back down to earth, to wander irresponsibly,
and, on occasion, look up at the skies in wonder.

Marilyn Kallet

Cons

Don't con a conwoman, Euridice lipped.
   The gig she hired Orpheus for was cushy,

touch of sweat, some nights.
   Liar and lyre, she thought.

Eury was into bad boys long after her
   Retired Underground Groupie pin arrived.

She was paying the big O a stud fee,
   though there was no *shtupping* involved.

Just singing. He could belt a lyric.
   If eagles boomed like Pavarotti,

that would be him. His footing sure
   as any mountaineer. And his hair

made Eurydice want to tumble backward
   into hell, never mind the eons

it had taken hand-over-hand to climb out.
   She wanted to scale him

but that could happen only
   in measured sighs.

What could she offer him
   besides overtime?

Eternity is in love with the
   productions of time and honey,

he was a show-stopper.
   Encore! She plunged again and again,

like her skin.
   If she had trapped him in her

descent-into-personal-hell
   work-study program

he was agile enough to scale
   out, leaving her

rock bottom,
   her bottom no rock,

sagging in her capris,
   in an downturned

economy, her only skill
   an ancient come-hither look

that used to make cocks cry
   & point like weathervanes.

Storm Warning

I am the queen of a rainy country
whose king has gone dark.
He's a speechless river,
but I have not stopped listening.

The king left his voice somewhere else,
holds his cruelty close.
I have not stopped listening—
thunder, roar of the rising river.

More wall. His cruelty
huge and other-worldly.
The swollen river breaches the banks.
Indifferent gaze behind the weather.

He is the sullen king of elsewhere.
I am queen of a country where the wall is gathering.

The Love that Moves Me

amor mi mosse . . .

Makes me speak. Or is this
some lesser muse, that he-beast
with reeking innards?

Goth, I know!
Why call for answers
if love's divine?

Why not worship like *el maestro,*
a glimpse of his beloved?
Beatrice cupped vision in words.

Virgil spoke up.
Had he held still
there would have been no book,

no hell, heaven, souls.
Now every church in Florence
has their number, every schoolgirl.

I'm well past the middle of my life,
less able to cast visions
on a still life.

I won't scold.
Let's admire the blank
you have created,

the sea of silence that surrounds you,
the taciturn mountain
you climb daily.

I won't ask for hello.
That would show lack of faith.
Let the song be my mojo,

the *terza* save me from wraiths,
rima not take me down.
Be my Virgil if not my angel.

If not my divine *amor,*
I might settle
for gutsy love.

Helga Kidder

Listening

As day wipes perspiration off her forehead,
the evening star a rogue in the sky,
I listen to sourwood and sweet gum leaves.
They rustle and moan songs of an ancient sea
below, murmuring, steering millennia,
as if expatriates, through the valley.

Ignited by trappers one hundred years ago,
this foothill burned to the ground, invited
deciduous riff-raff that now climbs to the top,
brambles beneath scrappy fir. Trunks mottled gray,
limbs arthritic, trees cling to the seasons
at the whim of developers.

Possums, squirrels scatter as trails are hewn,
tracts dug into the hill to embrace dwellings.
Next summer youngsters will climb branches
and teens carve their first love inside a heart.
Trees will continue to shelter and shade,
hide sadness in their tangled underworld.

This evening they shake their heads and sigh.
I sigh with the trees. Time slowly closes the door.

W. F. Lantry

Williams Was Right

As if, already in this frosted dawn
these stars had drawn away all warmth, as if
the patterned constellations broke their rounds
conceding, in the luminous vast space
of absolute cold, something colder still,
this ice sketches new figures over glass

reminding me of snowdrifts on the banks
of northern rivers—one particular
bridged every quarter mile near its bay
that in my mind seems universal now,
a wilderness of concrete and bent steel
reflecting architectural conceits

or archives, meant to imitate the sky's
own curves, or ice-ridges cutting my hands,
or waterfalls, caught by a sudden wind
as if these constant fluxes could be stilled
or some new form be reinvented to
rename the figures of our early dawn.

Michael Levan

Walking through the Weeds off Number Ten

Walking through the weeds off number ten
I found my ball, a shanked drive, nestled
under the chin of a dead deer. Judging by size,
it couldn't have been much older than a fawn—

or maybe it was, and I couldn't tell the difference.
I've never been familiar with animals,
how they graduate to adulthood.
These matters have never had easy explanations.

I reached out the head of my three-iron,
tried to retrieve what I'd lost there,
but I poked too far, jammed the steel edge
into the dark mass at the deer's throat.

Then, like a daisy's first petals
after a long winter, maggots sprouted
from the wound, writhed in the red-caked down,
squirmed for cover in the untrampled grass.

My father called to me. We had to play on.
I looked into the deer's eye, imagined it still
clear and brooding, knew what I had to do:
I left the ball, scuffed and stained green, a sign

someone had lost, and walked to the first cut of rough.
I dropped another, perfectly white, on the grass,
played it for three holes until one angry swing cut
the dimpled shell, made it common and unclean.

Beginning with a Line by W. S. Graham

At night. And here I am descending and
there is so much that whispers and calls
will not answer. I find this more and more
perfect the way it lights water
rippling underneath the bridge's trusses
in such fair and even waves,
and all those cars fumbling slowly
into midnight's blue-black memory.
When will I remember them again,
when will they demand to be taken
back into the present?
                              Maybe enough time
has passed for me to begin
forgetting when I was young and
purposeful and spent so many hours
fumbling to replace myself with her love
under a willow's sad embrace.
Or when I lay in bed and tried
to hear what my blood sounded like
inside me. Maybe enough has changed
for me to believe this night, stars
and moon descending ever steady and
perfect will be my only memory
worthy of return, that won't
black and blue me like so many fists
I have curled myself into.

Judy Loest

Mythopoesis

Once in a tea shop in Chinatown, a poem by Li Po
Floated under counter glass. After one line—
In the land of Wu the mulberry leaves are green—winter
Became spring, three thousand miles suddenly no more
Than the length of a silkworm's cocoon unwound
Po's Wen-yang River was my Little Moccasin,
His Wu Valley my Moccasin Gap, just another
Remote province in Appalachia.   All those years
I managed to sentimentalize the useless things,
Our little hollow eroded between cedared hills,
The mulberry tree dropping its fat, black berries
Outside our kitchen door, the crude, unpainted house,
Its front porch on stilts with no stairs, like a dream
In which something is lost but there is no way back.
When the clerk, watching me read, said mulberry
links heaven and earth, its leaves are food for silkworms,
I thought of those Chinese women laboring
To make silk for the emperor and then of my mother
In her own land of Wu, articulating ambition
In quilt squares, the Singer's hum a bee's drone,
Color splashing the sad linoleum, how she leaned
Over her new and wondrous machine with calm resolve
To outrun poverty, foot upon the pedal, silencing God.

Mother-of-Pear Button

Cold as a fragment of bone, you blossom
In a box of rusty coins, catching the last
Light in the junk shop, promising to tell
Me the story I never knew and need
To remember. For instance, how the young
Woman who could have been my grandmother
Might have chosen cotton over silk, thinking
Of the journey ahead, and as a consolation
Bought you on a card of four for a dime,
A prudent woman's brooch, a touchstone
She fingered later in the strange land,
Remembering the forsaken parlor
With its piano and china figurines.

But that would be a fabrication, the made up
Meal of history's orphan, hungry all the time.
The truth is, my grandmother could never
Afford you, as foreign as the Italian cameo
In the jeweler's window or the illusive dime
Itself, promising something as fundamental
As coffee or cornmeal, a pound of beans.

I buy you for her, who died at forty-three
On the Poor Farm in Wise, Virginia, leaving nothing
But a hand-tinted photograph, her plain wool
Dress as bereft of ornamentation as the cornfield
Behind her, stripped of its tasseled silk. In my dream,
I thread the needle and say, *Here, let me.*

Denton Loving

How to Grow Wildflowers or Dream #317

I soared in a dugout canoe that knew
its own path. My only companion
was a knowing crow who spoke
from my shoulder. The road is open,
he said, and it was. We sailed smoothly
over rough rapids and mountain
trails. Some force propelled us deeper
and faster. This is trust, the crow
said, when the road holds no signs,
when all sense of direction is lost,
when hopes have burst into flames.
Only blackened limbs and ashes
line back into the past. Hold trust
like a garden hoe, pull away the rocks.
Loosen the packed earth beneath. Let
wildflowers grow where you step,
chicory and birdfoot violets, black-eyed
susans and heartleaf.

Jacquelyn Malone

Revival at Diana Church of Christ

Nights when our thighs stuck to benches
and candleflies beat powdery wings
on churchhouse screens and the preacher said,
"Not one of you is righteous. No, not one,"

did any of us appear cocksure?
The fly specks on the ceiling burned darker,
and the two rows of white globes, hanging from chains
above the pews, slumped to melting points, heat

and God in the same space. In their limp dresses
the two Robertson girls beat time on their bosoms
with funeral home fans, and the songleader's hand,
as he wiped his palm across his chest,

left a damp outline on his shirt, as though
the pores of his soul were purged.
I'll tell you the truth, if truth is the point.
We were all afraid of God, and the strict hymns

nudged us on—songs red with sin, red
with blood—and before us His white throne,
incandescent, like a molten law judging us,
until our prayers were singed in the flame.

Michael O. Marberry

Night-Fishing

Waist-deep in the water of a creek, they'd wade.
Beneath their feet, the umber sand and gravel sank,
and steps sucked loose museums of forgotten things:
green pennies used to weigh a line, dead bugs, dead

leaves, and guts of lures that looked like nightcrawlers.
They'd heard all the snakes of the world were born
in the surge of scales that stretched from bank to bank,
that a yellow cat beneath a log might latch and drag—

swallow whole a man or child, if the moon was right.
Behind them, on the surface, skimmed the seine.
It might be morning before the farmer smelled smoke
from their camp, and came to find bones they'd left

on rocks, arranged like hood ornaments. If it was dark,
they'd bolt for the fields and feast on crickets and corn
right off the stalk. They'd hide till dawn, or till the man
gave up the ghost and rode home, whichever came first.

Namesake

with a line from Melville

He was mean-like: the type to pinch
a baby till it cried, stomp a sleeping dog,
and finger a girl so her sister felt it.

They said his hands were strong enough
to peel men like ripe fruit, bend railroad
spikes to ribbon, and rend days in layers

like some stubborn Southern Achilles.
He gave your brother free food and drink
at the station he owned—two or three

free shots at the punch-box con lottery,
or at the nickel slots, till the law caught on.
They called him Mr. Ben. It must've been

a mean twist that he hated you so much,
and that you hated him but wore his name.
Isn't that the way the world works? Life,

all of it, spinning against the way it drives.
When he died, they said he was mid-swing
and shouting—all *et up* inside like stale bread,

hard and gut-moldered. *Bad heart*, the doc said.
And everyone agreed: some folks better off
dead. To that, even the preacher said *Amen.*

Jeff Daniel Marion

Song for the Wood's Barbeque Shack in McKenzie, TN

Here in mid-winter let us begin
to lift our voices in the pine woods:

O sing praise to the pig
who in the season of first frost
gave his tender hams and succulent shoulders
to our appetite:

praise to the hickory embers
for the sweetest smoke
a man is ever to smell,
its incense a savor
of time bone deep:

praise for Colonel Wood and all his workers
in the dark hours who keep watch
in this turning of the flesh
to the delight of our taste:

praise to the sauce—vinegar, pepper, and tomato—
sprinkled for the tang of second fire:

praise we now say for mudwallow, hog grunt, and pig squeal,
snorkle snout ringing bubbles of swill in the trough,
each slurp a sloppy vowel of hunger,
jowl and hock, fatback and sowbelly, root dirt and pure
piggishness of sow, boar, and barrow.

American Primitive: East Tennessee Style

Hearing the screech
of a gate come open
and the click as the latch
snaps back into place
lights up whole rooms
inside me.
       First the rain barrels outside
one at each corner of the house
both rusty—
the ice 2 inches thick,
risen above the edge
and glistening.
       Then inside.
A Warm Morning heater
to bake your backside
(on top a tin can, stripped
of its label,
holding water to give the room
its proper atmosphere).
Behind on the wall
McDonald's Mill Calendar,
its bottom curled upward from
too many warm mornings
but standing as a sentinel
of weather for the day,
holiday, sunrise, moonphase,
best planting time
or just
plain days gone by.

At the Wayside

Coming back in the fall dark
somehow I still expect to find
it the same: enter through
a screen door & there you are
lodged behind the counter, taking
arms against the last remaining
flies, swatter in hand
& eyes focused on the stock
market pages, dreaming of gold & Cadillacs.
Already at 14 that very day
our dreams had rounded to perfection:
the Yankees win again & Don Larsen
has pitched the perfect game:
now it is the evening
Speedy turns full volume on the radio
replaying each strike, the blast of voices
beside the steaming black coffee on the counter
till he forgets the paper route that has mapped
35 years of his life.
It is the evening Buford Ray
leaves 5 games racked on
the pinball, leaps onto the counter
beside the radio, his hands cupped
to his mouth & puts Johnny Weismuller
to shame in the best Tarzan yell
this side of the Roxy Theatre.
It is the evening Donnie Roy gooses
the waitress Evelyn Lee in the ribs,
frogs her arm & spins her out onto
the floor near the jukebox where already
Buford Ray has slugged the juke
as the Kitty Wells record whines,
the overhead fan whirls,
and the dancers spin & spin & spin with the world,
the sound of feet, music, hands clapping
going out into the dark
searching the distances of stars & moon
until finally Mrs. Mapes looks up
over the stock market section of her *Journal*
& for the first time in nearly 15 years
a broad grin stretches her wrinkled cheeks
before she smacks her swatter on the cash

register and says, "Now boys."
And now I enter.

A face I've never seen before
rises, floats moon-like in the mirror
behind the register.
Youth glistens in the hard light,
disguised only by a blond mustache:
"What for you, good buddy?"
"Change—change for a dollar," I say,
squinting into the light,
"just some change."
Past a still overhead fan,
past a door no longer screened,
I turn back to the waiting
dark, cold & starless.

Linda Parsons Marion

Genealogy

Here is your bloodpath, I tell my father, compass
of kith and kin. I've lost touch, he says, it's all
I can do to find tomorrow.

Plotting our course since 1745, to King George's
lands in Lunenburg, Virginia: Thomas Parsons,
Elizabeth, and four of their twelve set minds on Tennessee.
Dollie to Jasper to Garner to Joel to Martha to John
Wesley (on my Methodist side) to Arthur, I am
the eighth boot up this ladder's rung.

Cousins, twice and five times removed, I unearth
lamplight and featherbed, your calling away
from sweetly known ground. With Shawnee
scouts, were you caught by late snow fording
the Gap, longboat driven to teeth of the shoals?
Was it elbow room you hankered for, a restless
pushing on, the frontier open as a question?

Along rutted roads, these lost shadows meet
our tomorrows with huzzahs, yellow flash
swung as welcome to enter, take rest and mead.
I bow to Ulster reels stashed in ship's hold,
lament beloveds taken by typhus or musket.
Your book of years is my groaning board,
bracelet braided from wilderness and rivers
crossed, ring around our new-rooted tree.

Mac

You see the rounder most in the sepia photo,
hat cocked over one eye, pranking with brothers
Owen and Ivan, bad boys of the old Hartsville
school. You can almost see the outline of bronze
glass held close, voluptuous curve already thunder
in his young Ulster blood. When he leaves the scarce
inheritance of a tobacco farm, his stepfather decent
but still not his daddy, the beacon of cigarette so casual
in my grandfather's hand lights the road to Nashville's
New South. Brass doors open to bankers and merchants
flush with capital, contractors unrolling blueprints
of the marbled Acropolis. Only at the chiseled columns
and Olympian pediment are there scraps for a farmboy
whose veneer buckles under drink and hardship,
four stairstepped daughters, a wife who has forsworn
his bed. His fine chances to measure lumber
in an ironed shirt or barber at the Maxwell House
traded for a sometimes job in the Arcade's catacombs,
a shady corner where no one comments on the bottle
shoved to the side or behind the counter,
all the white worlds traded for another swig
at that sweet-burning fountain.

Wanderlust

A swat of the Welsh wind scuttled you
down the Swansea coast, already the world traveler.
In London hostels you lived on tins of beans
and tomatoes, one eye peeled for mice and punk
thieves. That summer you shared a flat
with New Zealanders above the chocolate shoppe,
arranged lemon tarts in paper buntings
for the festival goers, Edinburgh's midnight
sun playing brilliantly on.

You return to Tennessee foothills arched
and licking your ankles, though soon tire
of it all—this insignificant house, nursery rocker
in the attic stained with hours we sailed

hungering under the cheddar moon, friends
whose folded pictures you carried on the Tube—
hometown baggage a sinker's weight
luring little worth remembering.

In my mind, you say, I'm *over there*.
Maybe you'll move to New York or Charleston,
someplace not Knoxville, not *here*.
Just when your heels settle into purple phlox
and the lilacs ripen, when *home* thrums
a steady, almost forgotten rain, the far
distance opens its heaven.

Child of cities and rural parts, cobbled
and crooked streets, daughter born under
the fierce bull, sign you will go where you will.
With no one to warn you of lake's shoulder,
alley, uncovered well, journey these homeroads
until time to set out again. Until then
pack light, intent on the song of here
and there, the rough seeds of becoming
tucked under your tongue.

Clay Matthews

The Electric Bill

Evening shadows, the telephone wires grow long
against the dusk. The phone rings. I wait on the bed
for something to happen, the ceiling seems like such a long way
away. There's a little boy in the field out back
who doesn't listen when his mama calls. There's a rusted Buick
in the neighbor's yard that won't turn over. We bloom. We decompose.
We measure time in car batteries bought at the auto parts store.
Gasoline drips into puddles in the asphalt. The old couple
at the service station eats crackers while their grandchild
watches the newest cartoon. The news. The news is terrible.
We persist. We don't believe you. In small towns like this one,
everyone knows everything about everybody, which isn't much
of anything. I would pick a flower, but they're not growing.
I would the stars come out, but it rains. Every fall they cut
the limbs off the trees here, they cut them down to the trunk,
down to the elbows. Springtime the maples return and grow round.
We give birth to a thousand dreams. Oh, we wish. The electric trucks
stop to raise their ladders. Everyone else just reaches for the sky.

Transactions

The hyacinth is almost done, and the sun
comes over the mountains. Morning, y'all.
Empty trash canisters lined along the street,
the gutters just trickling now, I had a dream
last night and then I remember a storm,
the dog jumping up beside me on the bed.
So, maybe go ahead and fear the reaper.
It begins here. Seeds in the ground, turnip
greens and wild onions coming up
through the neighbor's garden. The window
shook. I didn't. Then two crows came
down into a tree, and I thought
how March can make a mad fool
of even the darkest bird. What did I expect?
$77 on the Lucky 7 scratch-offs.
The train whistle to play me a tune.
I killed a wasp yesterday and didn't really
want to, but my daughter scoots across
this house now, I felt responsible, I felt sad,
I really didn't feel much of anything at all.
The potted plants get dry, and we water them.
The trees fill out the electric lines.
Somewhere out there a bank is opening
its doors. And I'm not saying I'm right.

Andrew McFadyen-Ketchum

Corridor

Drunk, we wound our way up the wind-bent
stilts that rose from the old Marathon Building,
abandoned in the days long after our father's
fathers milled cotton and women bobbed
their hair—each step skyward reporting
in the hollow iron we ascended. From there
the world swayed with the wind and our tinny echo,
our legs hung out over the lip of the city, scissor-
kicking at the night. From there we could cradle
that city in our palms: the big rigs and V-6s
swinging by on the s-curves of I-40, a pair
of spotlights probing figure-eights in the clouds
over downtown, the projects playing their music
of rebuilt Chevy Novas and catcalls and bass.
When I return home, I pass that water tower.
During the day, it stands. Yielding. Nothing.
At night though, I've seen kids climb
that long cold corridor to the celestial, the red
glow of cherries passed back and forth
like a pair of taillights winding their way west
down a late mountain road—pulsing, breaking,
another sharp turn on that half-moon landing—
those above having risen with such ease
above the rooftops and steeples, the switchbacks
of the Cumberland no longer obscured
by hackberries and fog, the dim illuminations
of billboards no longer hovering overhead
like messages from the future. More than once
I've thought of returning to that high vantage
point, stood at its base and planned my climb—
daylight not yet flickered out like a bulb, the stars
waiting to tend their signal fires. But I always
turn away and return the way I've come.
I already know how darkness folds over us,
the fear that comes with hard wind unbroken
by rain. I already know that city, pressed
like an ember in the amber of its own light
and so certain of its being.

Driving into the Cumberland

We knew we weren't the first or the last, clanging along
in our clambake of 30-weight and red-lined RPMs, Pete weaving
in and out of the US 100's metered yellow dashes. We were sixteen,
fifteen miles west of town above that sheer drop of Tennessee
limestone, where, gas pedal weighed down with a cinderblock
and shifter shifted into D, we watched that V-6 peel out
in a sidewinder of mud clods and black exhaust to somersault

eighty feet to the Cheatham County Cumberland below.
These were the days before death and finances would have stopped us
back at the fork in the highway; the days when we still compared
the putting on of a condom to suiting up for the moon
and were angry with our fathers for being our fathers.
I still think it was all the unknowing that sixteen years of living
had allotted us that drove us to that promontory,

the Continental's lone headlamp coppering as it sank
in the waters made murky by run-off, like a submersible.
To watch it disappear around a bend in the river and know
for fact we'd left our mark on the city of our births
where, story claimed, countless Cutlass Sierras and GTOs
had come to rest over the decades in a mausoleum of cracked
manifolds and snapped steering columns in the shallow waters

of the riverfront eight blocks from our high school. *What was it
about that Continental that just begged to fly?* we'd ask all summer,
rewriting the details of our story beyond even our own disbelief:
how, staying in the car, we tossed back the last dregs of our fifths
of Tequila, yelled *fuck it!*, and floored that once-luxury four door,
racing for the edge. What song Billy Corgan chirred

through the radio changed hands in the telling innumerable
times; what degree of fullness the moon we were wise enough
not to remember. What mattered was how we swam
by its baleful light back to shore and lay there laughing, breathing.
What mattered was what we saw on the long walk home:
The world, Pete kept saying. *We're finally seeing the world.*

Anne Meek

October, Knoxville

headlights pinched
by the fog into stars
ragged monarchs
faltering, skidding
out of control into the ditch

infinite scallops of oak
leaves, green into red,
relentless footfall, leaves
walking on leaves,
our soft steps ask questions

all night long hickory nuts
hit the roof with the
certainty of winter,
startling us with staccato
answers: ka-pow, ka-pow

next day we gather them
they all look alike
and we've forgotten
which questions
they answered

Elijah Rene Mendoza

Athens of the South

Cement Parthenon near the four-star hotel,
downtown high rise apartments where the homeless beg,
expensive steak, land-locked sushi and coffee shops:
regentrification south of the Mason-Dixon.

East Nashville, Cashville,
where the college kids don't go.
Thugs on the porch skipping school
watch cars with spinning rims
bump music from trunk speakers,
Don't fuck with the Dirty South.

Off in Nolensville, the Kurds, the Mexicanos, the immigrants
fight for territory like I-440 is the new frontier,
but every block has a taqueria next to a Waffle House,
and the place with a painted Greek Flag
sells gyros with French fries.

Tennessee Titans from Texas
and Jack Daniels at the sports bar.
Country music spelled CMT on the skyline,
but the white kids listen only to hip-hop.
Pride in the Southwestern Bell tower.
Another Cracker Barrel restaurant.

The Belle Meade plantation is a museum,
finally. The tour of Andrew Jackson's house
asks you to remember the servants.
Downtown by the karaoke bar and neon cowboy boot,
there's the store that can order any UN-recognized flag.

Nashville, named for Revolutionary war hero Francis Nash.
Athens, Greece, wasn't built in a day;
it was built by slaves over centuries of war.
On the banks of the Cumberland
running through downtown,
a new South rises every night.

Joanne Merriam

Larix laricina Anaphora

Consider the hackmatack, the tamarack, its comical asymmetry.
Its whirled clusters of needles. Its hundred hidden chickadees.
The hundred hidden chickadees' down-slurred anaphoric whistlings.

Consider its yard, the yard's poverty, the spare automobile parts.
The free-range child, shirtless, shoeless, her mother at work,
her father sobbing inside the house, her dead brother still dead.
The tangled mass at the edge of the lot, the whirled clusters of daisies.
The whirled cluster of daisies leaning against the gutted lawnmower.

Consider the small yellow boots lying on their sides under the porch.
The past that can't be altered. That keeps repeating.
The ghosts of hackmatacks squatting in the mist.
The mist's conquest of every view.

Corey Mesler

Fathers of Daughters

One of the things they
don't tell you
is that you will dress and
undress Barbie
thousands of times.
You will pull tight dresses
over impossibly
shapely hips, wrap bras
no bigger than wasps
over perfectly
mounded breasts, as hard
as algebra. They
don't tell you you
will suffer the feminine;
you will structure and
restructure it inside yourself.
And, if you spent enough
time there earlier,
when you were stronger,
it doesn't help.
They don't tell you
it will break your everloving heart.

Beverly Acuff Momoi

She asks me if I believe

in Jesus, halfway between Memphis and Whiteville.
Her right eye is filled with blood. Dogwoods lace
the lawns, their rust-edged petals a reminder. Nine days

to another Good Friday. Eleven and she will celebrate
Easter. Her face, a crumpled tissue of pain, turned
to catch the twists of kudzu and honeysuckle tangled

in the trees. In front of every country church, signs
in black and white. The only sound: tires against pavement,
relentless hum of righteousness and reckoning.

R. B. Morris

The University of Tennessee Revisited

How weird to walk the halls of a university again
A stranger, a spy I am
Not only the dropout, the outsider
But also from another time
A different day of learning
My one poor year spent burning
     the candle for peace
Staging a strike, studying the people,
       dodging police
William Knustler, Phil Ochs, Circle Park
Billy Graham, Dick Nixon, Neyland Stadium
No nostalgia for me
I learned a few things

It was all in passing
And still passing it seems

But don't I carry with me some of those days
And some from long before?
I learned something early on
I found it in daydreams and broken crayons
The melody of sky and earth
A hidden voice
The hot breath of running free
And what good has it done me?
And what of all those pages turned
     and paths gone down?

I became a cloud dreamer, book reader,
   soul singer
A sun chaser and great loafer
Like Adam in the garden

Like Whitman in America
A student of the stone
I called myself those many moons ago
Upon the eve of leaving formal schooling

Nearly 30 years now rolling that stone
And what can be said of all that AWOL?
Well, no regrets
None that I would mention
I've learned a few things
                a few things in passing
But one walk down that long echoed corridor
The painted block walls, the lockers
And all is recalled from before and after
The stone, the wall, the endless hallway out

Kevin O'Donnell

To a Runaway Truck Ramp

on Interstate 26, between Johnson City, Tennessee,
and Asheville, North Carolina

For years you have waited here,
dusted with snow in wintertime, and lined
with rills of gravel in spring.

In late summer
restless teenagers
in the middle of the night have ridden

S.U.V.'s to your crest
and echoed lonely yawps
off your dynamited walls of schist.

In the days to follow,
their tire tracks have led
interstate travellers to notice and wonder.

Until finally one October,
on a Tuesday evening, along the edge
between nightfall and dark,

an eighteen-wheeler, fully loaded,
owned and operated by a man
with too many bills and too little sleep

loses its air brakes
past the crest of the ridge
with a violent hiss,

and there, one thousand yards along,
in an explosion of gravel, the pilgrim
nestles in your arm—

the way a tear rides a cheek,
the way a bullet leaves a gun,
the way an arrow fits exactly in the wound.

Ted Olson

Crinoid Stem

"It looks like bamboo" was Sam's response,
"but really it's just some rock." I watched:
he placed a fossil on the counter
of the country store his father owned
long before the Second World War.
The voice of a local preacher moaned
from Sam's radio. I had a hunch:
life in some valleys has not changed much
since the "monkey trial," when John Scopes
taught students how to read signs like this.
The lesson, laughed at, did not take hold
here, as I'm now a living witness.
I stopped at Sam's Grocery to buy gas,
walked inside, waited behind a man
who was showing Sam what had been found
by a child at a construction site:
"Proof that God is great!" Both men bent down
as if in prayer. That theory was right.

Wilderness Road

Daniel Boone strolled
through weeds so high
he couldn't see

beyond the old
path. He passed by,
then climbed that tree:

wilderness flowed
toward a new myth,
our history.

"I'll build a road:
we'll all merge with
the mystery."

ಐ

He carved his name
in that rough bark,
smoothing the way

for those who came
to brave the dark—
or so they say:

Boon Cilled a Bar.
. . . A brag, to coax
settlers to stay

in the wild, far
from home? . . . A hoax,
one that would pay?

William Page

Skating

In our basement the furnace burned
the anthracite I shoveled into a hopper,
its worm gear grinding like a train.
My hair was black as the lumps of coal
and curly as gulping blades of the shaft
that chewed the freezing night into dawn.
I used long iron claws to lift the clinkers
of iridescent gray and violet.
Into a bucket I'd drop them and carry
them to a waiting row beside the driveway.
In the basement I'd watch Father,
the band saw's voice screaming
at the mounds piling on the bench.
The first day I strapped on my skates,
I cinched their jaws into my soles.
There was a silver key my father tied
to a shoelace I wore about my neck.
When I stood up, wheels turned to wings,
and I flew to my knees, my temple
missing the workbench by inches.
Father took my arms to help me up.
The disappointed workbench said nothing.
The floor lay with its blank stare.
The furnace loomed, provider
of the fires of Hell I'd heard the evangelist
scream about as he stoked our fears.
But a piece of coal cracked open, and out
spurted a flame bluer than my father's eyes.

Madame Le Coeur

If Death steals in as *Scripture* says,
why, put up a beacon and delay
your fate. But if the old boy comes
clowning like a nightclub comedian,
who could laugh off his grisly trick
more marvelous than any magician's?
Not *Sherwood Anderson*, sipping
a deadly sliver of toothpick
from his dry martini. Even
in fiction he didn't ask for this final
drink. Not *Friedrich Nietzsche*,
choking on a dish of delicious cream. For all
his philosophic erudition, he hadn't guessed
the secret word would be *dessert*.
Pity *Li Po*, his laughing eyes glazed over
with drunken splendor, who tripped
astern his little boat, trying to steal
a kiss from Mistress Moon's reflection,
and sank into Widow Lake's embrace.
Consider tragedian *Euripides*, whose
skull was split, thanks to a terrified turtle
plummeting from a clumsy eagle's grip,
or madcap *Rasputin* fatally turned morose
when he was poisoned, shot, and drowned.
Clever *Cleopatra*, who spoke
nine languages if you count asp,
found nothing amusing
in Death's ridiculous sting.
Even that celebrated French whore
Madame Le Coeur failed to giggle
when she slipped on a peach
and slid in through Heaven's boudoir door.

Randy Parker

Leaving Us

Our son molted like a field cricket, climbing
out of juvenile exoskeletons and leaving them
in piles behind the bathroom door.

He became ever more elusive, the
one chirping somewhere within our walls
but nowhere to be found.

And then he crept away, chirring
far afield, far afield, far afield,
stridulating effortlessly with cellular wings.

Charlotte Pence

Yard Meditation

He steps outside with his glass of water,
Settles into his lawn chair, and stares
At the shell-white sky: hazy, humid—constant.
Each day he loses more the expectation
That all will better itself; the gnat

That keeps poking, trying to sip
From the corner of his eye, will return,
Hover again in the background breeze
Of cicadas and I-40 traffic.

This is neither city nor country.
Neither today nor yesterday.
He thinks of his ex who called,
Can't remember what she said.
Instead: sliced wedges of a Pippin apple

She cut in her hand while they lay in bed,
Her thumb the knife's stopper; a strand
Of sunlight, spotted from window dirt,
Hitting her calf; same cicada

And highway humming around them.
One summer's end, they set out to find
The shack where his grandparents lived.
A day trip. Something to fill time.
Queen Anne's lace and ragweed

Flicked behind his knees as he trudged up
A stranger's hill to the shack still standing. Leaning.
Newspaper on walls curling down
Over the wrought-iron headboard.

And in the corner, a spider moving in.
Web open, unfinished, yet she wrapped
The gnat into a whitish bundle for later.
Her movements—something he'd seen before—
The fussing of hands over a kitchen counter,

Her sorting forks from spoons, sugar spoons
From tea spoons, tea spoons from soup spoons . . .
Then the pulling out of the drawer,
Darkness there, and long, open boxes.

Everything fitting into its own little space
As if no other option ever exists.

Divining

i.

We are a train, father and daughter, car and caboose, divining rods held in front of chests. We are water-witching, doodlebugging. Divining.

We are marching. I tell him we are ready to parade down Main Street. And I'll write our banner slogan: *Call Spike. He'll treat you right.* He says, *Shush. You have to feel it. Shush.*

So, I wait for the twitch, wait for the sticks to cross. To x. Follow his pace, head down, feet placed in eight-inch patterns. Listen to whatever it is that rides the wind. Butterfly. Apple. Old bell. Nothing. I am learning how to listen to nothing. More real than what is there. I hear his face sweating, the sticks not moving, the promise from earlier in the morning: *We'll get rich. You would like that, huh? Be like your friends.*

His stick rigs. Or doesn't. We stand so still I see how much everything moves in this yard: the leaves, the squirrels, the shrubs. We stand so still Dad says, *I can feel the ground soften. Water. There is water.*

Or maybe not. I realize we do not have a machine to drill a well—nor do we know what prevents a well from caving in. I can hear his face reddening, and so I tell him I don't want a well. I want what I have: a father who is a diviner.

ii.

Tell me a secret, I asked him later. *Tell me how you know where there is water.*

He said: *It's like you can fall down. And just drop and drop and drop. And no one or no thing is there to stop you.*

Like the girl who fell in the old well last summer and died? When all the news crews came out and camped by the hole?

No, not like that at all, he said. *She was one of the lucky ones. People didn't forget her.*

Emilia Phillips

Creation Myth

I wouldn't drink from the creek next to my house
that runs like a vein of old blood
to the Tennessee. Somewhere in Kentucky,
a poet is leading his congregation
in a service for the Church
of Elkhorn, but there's no god,
just a low mist standing in for the Holy Ghost,
just kayaks & wet suits on Sundays, & the day's
Collect taken from Byron or Shelley. *I ought to be
thy Adam*, the creature says to Frankenstein,
but the creature was never as pretty as the Adam
on the walls of the Church of the Holy Trinity
in Hrastovlje where a fault line waits beneath
its stone, waiting to open the earth like a bloom.
As a child, my grandfather ate dandelion
sandwiches, just weeds placed between Wonder
bread, when there was nothing else. I sat in chapel,
at my Episcopal school, watching the rain, wanting
the building to flood until we were stuck there living
off of communion crackers & paddling the halls
in canoes made of church pews. Even now,
as I sit on the bank of the creek, I root my feet
into the cool sludge & mud & touch
the healed rib that was broken years ago.

Strange Meeting

If my footprints could
be swept away,
if my fingerprints could
be wiped from everything
I've ever touched,
I'd be a thief, breaking
into my own home
to steal a stereo that plays
songs I used to know.

Outside, I'd pull my stocking
mask off, sit down
in the wet grass, unfurl the nude
sheer up my calve, & press
play. Maybe it's Bill Frisell,
Dave Holland, & Elvin
Jones lurking around a melody
in "Strange Meeting."

In place of singing, I'll smoke
A bummed clove cigarette
I've been holding onto
for something like this,
lean back against one
of the oak trees, watch smoke
rings I don't even know
how to make rise & break
among the leaves.

Maybe I'd ask you to join me,
an accomplice in a stolen dance,
because the wind is too still
& something needs to stir
the atmosphere into jazz.
I wish I could say I still
played horn, that my lips were full
from hitting high notes instead
of swollen from biting
them in this whole note, whole rest
gag order of the tongue.

I'll be as quiet as dust swept
under the bed. I'll be as dizzying
as leaves shimmying in midnight
wind. If I exhale in the right
direction, will that breath turn
into a gust on the other side
of the world, will it gather up
these notes like they were dandelion
seeds & scatter, sow them
in rain-soaked fields that I will
never see? If I breathe

heavily while your hands are on
my hips, will you close
your eyes, become flushed
in the cheeks, red
as the sound of sirens speeding
toward us, wailing out of tune?

David S. Pointer

The Scrapper

He used to fight under antler chandeliers
sharp in his trotting razors, the attack

rooster now roams through discarded
nail kegs, egg crates, and cream cans,

unadorned claws, rescued and retired fire
atop a wood pile big as an Amish wagon.

Michael Potts

Butterscotch

At a philosophy conference I sit near
the candy bowl on my table, enjoy
grape, cherry, strawberry (a little
philosophy on the side), and when I reach

butterscotch, I'm five years old
at Granny's, sitting in a ladder-back
chair, legs too short to dangle as Granny
sets down a bowl of butterscotch candy,

and I eat with eager zest, joy stretching
time until it becomes taffy. A yellow
schoolhouse light above centers a circle
of brightness surrounding, its reflection

quivering on the clear glass of a nearby
cabinet. Aunt Jean irons the day's laundry,
Godlight pouring in until it floods the linoleum
floor. Startled by applause, I'm back

at the conference; the world grows dim
and I sense joy slip like soap, my desperate
hands reaching again for butterscotch,
finding only space and glass.

Lynn Powell

July's Proverb

The shortest distance between what's gone and what's to come
is you. But that's neither here
nor there to the rabbit, plush
and quick in the rainsoft grass,
or to that taut bird, hotwired for song.

The noon sky acts as if nothing mauve has ever happened.
Clouds go on and on about the weather.
And soon enough, the delicate
hypocrisy of winter—snow falling all over itself
to wish you weren't here.

There's no wisdom in the windvane
and no help in that daytime moon,
slow, half-hearted, besieged by blue. Yet the mind
keeps watching from its shade of words—
the mind and its archangel, the flesh.

Original Errata

He thought He had made himself perfectly clear:
Let there be lust.

But where there's a will, there's a way
to misunderstand, to make tragic
puzzles of shame and fruit
from lovely ambiguities He had always felt.
No wonder He receded
farther than the stars, farther
than the white room of Emily Dickinson.

He'd had such hopes for the garden:
a slow eureka of tongues in understated moonlight,
rosy virtuosities at dawn, even the pink
loneliness at noon the right hand heals.

Thus, He greeted the first tenants
of the flesh, then paused beside the pear.

He wanted to confide a brazen sweetness—
the short, slippery slope
He had made for them
into love.

Melissa Range

High Lonesome

Tennessee November: nothing slumbers:
in the barn, bluebottles' ice-whittled shells
hue the tops of feed and water buckets,

inlay corn shucks and tobacco flakes
instead of the lashes of Appaloosa or Paint.
Everything which could be salvaged

has gone to rot—a dead woman's house,
her dead husband's barn. I live
among the ghosts of horses I gave names,

the ghosts of ballads; the murders in the songs
murmur murder in my heart. Cold bronze, catgut,
furrows like stretched steel about to snap.

Tonight the barrel fire can't hold the heat
inside all that I hear: tobacco leaves—pendant,
tendoned from sticks in the hayloft—beat

a feeble percussion in the barn-breeze,
the leaves browned, unsold, brittle
as the light the hay holds in its cells.

Black sky gashes black hills; black wind
yowls past the hayloft door, snags
on sweetgum and poplar, clawhammer-branches

marking snow—a break in the sky
as a voice might break to falsetto,
as when old-timers' fiddles

bow the center of my throat,
the chokepoint where the salt and cold
collect, the moment when I have to sing

or crack. The holler thrums its plaint
into the wind, the ground, the frets
that net the mountains to the sky.

The season at its coda refuses to go out
quiet, shrills its endings till they twang
and clash. Storm might come, might pass.

O constant sorrow, O murderous love,
O resting place of the name that dies with me—
outside, the pine trees frail the sky to ash.

Flat as a Flitter

The way you can crush a bug
or stomp drained cans of Schlitz out on the porch,

the bread when it won't rise,
the cake when it falls after the oven-door slams—

the old people had their way
to describe such things. "But what's a flitter?"

I always asked my granny. And she could never say.
"It's just a flitter. Well, it might be a fritter."

"Then why not say 'fritter'?"
"Shit, Melissa. Because the old people said 'flitter.'"

And she smacked the fried pie into the skillet,
and banged the skillet on the stove,

and shook and turned the pie
till it was on its way to burnt.

Flatter than a flitter, a mountain
when its top's blown off:

dynamited, shaved to the seam,
the spoil pushed into hollers, into streams,

the arsenic slurry caged behind a dam,
teetering above an elementary school.

The old people said "flitter." They didn't live to see
God's own mountain turned

hazard-orange mid-air pond,
a haze of waste whose brightness rivals heaven.

When that I was a little bitty baby,
my daddy drove up into Virginia

to fix strip-mining equipment, everything
to him an innocent machine in need.

On God's own mountain,
poor people drink bad water, and the heart

of the Lord is the seam of coal gouged out
to fuel the light in other places.

The old people didn't live
to give a name to this

kingdom of gravel and blast.
Lay me a hunk of coal

on my flittered tongue
to mark the mountains' graves,

to mark my father's tools
quarrying bread for my baby plate,

to mark my granny slapping dough
as if with God's own flat hand.

Crooked as a Dog's Hind Leg

Yanking my lank hair into dog-ears,
my granny frowned at my cowlick's
revolt against the comb, my part

looking like a dog's shank
no matter what she did, crooked
as the dogtrot path

out the mountain county I left
with no ambitions to return,
rover-minded as my granddaddy, crooking

down switchbacks that crack the earth
like the hard set of the mouth
women are born with where I'm from.

Their faces have a hundred ways to say
"Don't go off," "Your place is here,"
"Why won't you settle down?"—

and I ignored them all like I was one
of their ingrate sons (jobless, thankless,
drugged up, petted to death), meandering

like a scapegrace in a ballad,
as a woman with no children likes to do,
as a woman with crooked roots knows she can.

"When you coming home?" my granny
would ask when I called, meaning "to visit"
but meaning more "to stay,"

and how could I tell her
that the creeks crisscrossing
our tumbledown ridges

are ropes trying to pull my heart straight
when it's a crooked muscle,
its blood crashing in circles?

Why should I tell her
that since I was a mop-headed infant
and leapt out of my baby bed,

I've been bent on skipping
the country, glad as a chained-up hound
until I slipped my rigging?

What could I say but "I'll be home Christmas,"
what could I hear but "That's a long time,"
what could I do but bless

the crooked teeth in my head
and dog the roads that lead all ways
but one?

Sam Rasnake

A Certainty and Not the Poem I Meant to Write

> *If there is only one world, it is this one*
> —Larry Levis, "Decrescendo"

Rain, sounding like talk, like the dulled necessary words
of couches, of fireplaces and coffee tables, will be snow
by afternoon, and I will have forgotten the six crows,
the one mockingbird over the gnarled ridge.

I used to say I wouldn't bother with hidden things,
but now I need them too much—like a trumpet craves
the ballad. I ache for railroad underpasses,
lit houses, closed windows, shelves of books.

Dawn, wet and cold, shakes through the spruce on the hill.
The apple gives no note, acts hard of hearing, not willing
to show any emotion. I know this wind and have felt
the air for it, have waited beside summer roads, wanting

only its freedom. I promised myself I would give it back,
but never did, swallowing instead. I used to walk on whispers
through town, unwilling to let anyone know my secrets.
An empty lot, the one television station. The upstairs

bowling alley that rumbled over a bakery counter—
fluorescent pastries behind glass. The bus terminal,
abandoned, merciless, with its wall of magazines and
delicious, forbidden photographs. I could dream of cars

then, the shaking of my bed—a radio under my pillow—
horse-print curtain, brown and wild in the opened window,
giving way to such dark immovable skies over my own
desperate vocabularies of the smallest detail.

I knew nothing then. I asked no questions then,
but believed my life would always be as it was—
burning, ready at any moment, for something.
Now those streets are lost to me.

The legs I thought would swell forever,
would burn always, are dry, are tired, finished,
though I don't remember when this happened.
The streets I walk are only streets, nothing more.

They lead in circles, are under construction,
their cul-de-sacs invite no one.
Rain, according to local weather, boasts of flood,
but brings nothing. My streams are lost among thickets

of maple, oak, among fence posts, wire & rocks
& ditches where two horses, heads to the ground,
their powerful jaws undisturbed
in the world of grasses, prove their own design.

The streams push against my banks,
deliberate in what is given. Water rises
past my calves, my thighs, stomach, nipples, chin.
I flare both nostrils,

taking in this one last thing
my life brings. And then my eyes—
What I see there in the slow darkness is
exactly what I've wanted.

Mountain Verse

Someone tried to build a fence here,
a line that says there is always the *other*.
The one post is dislodged.

                                           Under stands
of pine & spruce & chestnut, water pours
from some dark certainty of earth
with deep smells of myth in its belly,

                                                  spills
down the ridge a soaked quilt of stones,
smooth and moss-covered.

                                      Past rusted wire
that spans the creek, mountain laurels lift
hosanna from the cool tangles of green and brown,
empty their bodies to this holiness, into a dust of sky
that settles its waiting down steep walls of blue,
as perfect an afternoon as can be lived.

Anne Delana Reeves

Lona's, Highway 50

Custer's *Last Stand* tilts above the jukebox.
Patsy Cline dreams. The Indians advance.
Behind the bar, Carla licks her bad leg
And whines after every sad country song.
At a table we sit and drink our beers,
You lean so close our heads almost touch.
We talk about love, but love won't last.
In a jar, red pickled eggs float like hearts.

Silos

Apparitions, the silos seem,
Sheathed in purple-hued clouds
Of dust from siphoned grain,
The sun low-pitched and parceling
Fields bundled in rolled bales.
Near a fence line of ragged pines
And the churchyard's stone wall,
Set years ago by poor Irish hands,
Bees swarm the split of a cedar,
Its needled limbs candled skyward.
The bees' velvety hum dims
And will be gone by winter.
I trail behind my dogs
Through the Garden of John
To read the shining stones:
War dead, mothers, daughters.
No one I know. The dogs listen
And nose the long narrow mounds,
Then paw the dirt for trembling moles.

J. Stephen Rhodes

American Gothic

We had a drawing once of a bedroom, pen and ink.
Through a window, leafless trees, a barn, fields covered with snow.
Inside, a brass bed, quilt, pile of pillows, two pairs
of shoes side by side under the foot rail, and a woven rug
on the floor, the oblong kind that winds out from its core.

Our marriage had, I'd thought, everything in its place, too—
soft surfaces, a window on the world we were in
but not of, somehow, onto the farm we'd bought, blanketed
with annual whites. We tried so hard I suspect I would
have stood out front with wire-rimmed glasses and a pitchfork,

if it would have helped. Perhaps we should have put candles
in front of the sketch. We did hang a stocking for Jesus,
read aloud to each other at night, and opened our doors
to strangers, thereby entertaining angels unawares,
which came to describe our selves, straining to get everything right.

Joshua Robbins

Sparrow

A man doubles over
      to fit the angled crawl space
            beneath the overpass,

his makeshift shelter against January,
      its icy transfiguration of every last
            façade and exposed city surface.

Surely he signifies something
      more than that which two
            slumped shoulders and a sunken

chest might represent to those
      of us sleepless in surrounding
            subdivisions: the last unlit

match perhaps, which, when struck
      and held in the cup of a palm
            has everything to do with prayer.

This much we know: no one thing
      corresponds to any other.
            A midnight trucker's jake-braking

detonates soundwall concrete,
      and we lie awake cursing
            suburbia's toothless ordinances,

which comforts no one and is
      as useless as questioning
            the possibility of mercy,

that *His eye is on the sparrow.*
      What I remember are weeknights
            spent at church, how the derelicts

gathered below on benches
      and cold pavement looked up,
          and how, first, we circled

the upright, sang each verse
      and refrain. Only then
          would we open our doors.

Kristin Robertson

Bonfire

This could be what dying feels like,
here, at dusk, on Dockweiler State Beach,

so close to the blaze I could half-pivot
the sand and trust-fall in toward someone shouting

Cool hat! or *How about some frisbee?* from the other side.
Within these busted pallets and flames,

my dead uncle practices karate kicks,
same leg swift-striking the air like a snake's tongue,

then tai chi, white crane spreading its wings, his arms
open wide, like Zoroaster, summoning this fire

for me. Farther down shore, with smoke in my sleeves,
I stall, play Jenga with firewood. I sip from a red cup.

Under the last of the sun, pelicans barrel
toward the widening pupil of glittering ocean.

I hear my mother, back in Tennessee, at the screen door:
Play in the sandbox after dinner until you no longer

see your own hand in front of your face.
Then you must come in.

Bobby C. Rogers

William Eggleston

> To me it seems that the pictures reproduced here are about the
> photographer's home, about his place, in both important meanings of that
> word.
> — John Szarkowski, Introduction to *William Eggleston's Guide*

I'm sure I'm wrong about him, but it's always seemed like slumming to me, those
    lovely color photographs—quickly seen
shots of broken grave monuments and all manner of sun-scoured refuse, peeling
    billboards, delicately corroding
service station signs and boxcars parked on the siding, copper-tipped clouds
    against an indifferent sky—process prints
as lurid as circus posters. I wish they didn't seem so damn familiar. All of life is
    slumming, even if you don't believe
in anything more than method: take just one shot of each view, but condition
    your eye to capture countless views.

Everyone in Memphis can tell you Eggleston's been barred from the Lamplighter
    Lounge, one of those beer joints
over on Madison. You know the kind of place—50¢ pool table, Rock-ola juke box
    stuffed with Otis Redding sides,
a Pabst Blue Ribbon clock running fifteen minutes fast. How is your behavior so
    bad you can't darken the door
of a dive like that? Even a town as rough as this one should be handled with
    manners and grace. There's something to look at
in the saddest room. Beauty is best when it's accidental. I was brought up to act
    polite, and maybe I'm too fearful of getting barred

from the smoky rooms of Memphis, but it breaks my heart to be shut out of even
    the shabbiest place. How empty
if the only thing left to look at is your own looking in this world so mysteriously
    encoded into shape and color, where even a tawdry streetscape
is built of parts we've only happened upon and had no hand in making. Look at
    the assurance of beautiful things, how they pose
and preen and covet our looking. Such need is what renders a thing uncomely.
    We should seek the repose of the unlooked at
because nothing's ever beautiful that's not in some measure caught unawares.
    And rust, no matter what else it is, is red.

Lost Highway

you'll curse the day...
       —Hank Williams

Years after the fact, he would say it was just the right time to make a move when
       he was invited to come into the bank, but he could see his path

blocked by the bank president's son, a man his very age and already groomed to
       rise. So he clung to the safe job. Too late to take anything back

the day the news came that the banker's son had died of a heart attack at the
       mahogany desk in his father's office. If our fates are fitted neatly

into the pans of a scale, it might have been anything that tipped the balance, any
       wrong turn or luckless cut of the cards, something as unlikely, even,

as losing the autograph—Elvis Presley coming down the driveway of Graceland in
       1958, braking a showroom clean Duo-Glide Harley

next to the cranked down window of his just as shiny Chevy Bel-Air, twenty-four
       payment slips left in the loan book. The singer called him *sir*,

wrote out an autograph and handed the scrap of paper to his wife, six-months
       pregnant with their first child, the sweet ending of a spring day spent

shopping and sight-seeing before the hour-long drive back to their teaching jobs
       in a Tennessee town hardly big enough to have use for a school.

Or when he was a boy, keeping still under a sweat-soured quilt, trying to hide
       from the polio virus settled in one leg's large muscles, the afternoon

of his highest fever, and through the unscreened window he could hear his
       parents reaching a decision on where to bury him. Might as well say

it all turned on the morning he was born, piercing the room with his first cried
       out description of what had befallen him, and every time

the wind nudged at the curtains, the room's shadows gave shape to a ragged
       patch of sunlight shifting its restless edges on the floorboards.

Lisa Roney

Violent Season

When I come in
from Florida gardening—
not really even gardening,
just keeping the yard—
I am dirty, shredded, and bruised.
I think a lot about wrestling gators,
feel almost as though I have been
doing some form of that,
though the only critters I've encountered
are anoles, frogs, and spiders,
all of them slithering
underfoot,
making the ground seem
like it's moving,
making me dizzy.
I think,
In the old country—Pennsylvania,
even muggy Tennessee—gardening seemed
somehow gentle.
It was something an amateur
could handle, something
pleasant (but for poison ivy).
Under a crisp sky,
I waited for the tulips and daffodils
to poke their way out,
tentative, curious.
The saw palmettos here resist
my trimming, claw me,
try to punch my eyes out.
Their stems crisscross in a malevolent
tangle and thrash knife-sharp edges
when moved aside.
The overgrown azalea,
now dead, crackles, but
does not let go of the sand.
It seems stronger dead than
it was alive.

Twenty or thirty buzzards devour
an armadillo
at the front curb
in under four hours.
It is gone, and
my skin
is blotched
with a prickly rash,
streaked with blood,
speckled from head to toe
with flecks of dark brown
earth spit.
In the cherished old places,
spring always threatened,
but threatened to leave,
to allow winter to return ferocious
in its absence.
But in Florida, spring
threatens
with its own violence.
It says,
While you think of the past
as a beloved old country,
I will cover you over
and rot you
in no time.

Jane Sasser

Dirge

A mouse is miracle enough to stagger sextillions of infidels.
—Walt Whitman

No one taught you how to die.
It was in you all along, like rummaging
for food, like burrowing through straw.
Clutching still the frail tendril of life,
you linger longer in your nest, days
blooming shorter and dimmer
like your eyes. Drifting into dreams,
you float through the gloaming
on an oak leaf raft, your body so light
scarcely your breath remains.
Oar then into dusk, small sharecropper.
Understand that the farm is bought,
the rope at its end, the candle snuffed.
Let Night close his great wings around you,
no predator after all, only softness like
nest feathers of home. Listen now:
it was always lullabies the stars sang,
your name the sweetest syllables they know.

Dim

And the burden is being smart enough to know
how dumb you are, to be aware of the thickness
of your fingers when you reach for a spool
of silk, to feel how your brain won't quite focus
when you look at numbers on a page,
and you wish you could pick up your glasses
and make it right. But there's no correcting
this haze—you have to go on living, knowing
you're a ninety watt bulb, there are dark
corners of you even you can't light.
So you slide into whiskey to dim
it on down, down into darkness you go,
that place you hope the brightness
of your dead brother's face won't touch,
blackness so deep you can't see the stricken
look on your daughter's face, the taut muscles
in your wife's turned back.

Horatio

Give me that man that is not passion's slave. (Hamlet 3.2.71-72)

Like each bereft messenger to Job,
bearing more news of slaughter and loss,
I alone am escaped to tell thee.
I was a shadow at that court.
Silence their tempests crashed against.
Good Horatio, they said, when they could
be brought to notice me at all, Good Horatio,
give Ophelia close watch. Watch my uncle.
If he react to the play, I'll know his guilt.
Thou art a scholar, Horatio. Speak
to the ghost. Make everything clear.
O Horatio, thou art e'en as just a man
as e'er my conversation coped withal.
As though justice were prized,
that cold blanket I tucked around
my heart. It was never my intent
to be philosophy made flesh,
with my nose buried in words,
while around me unfurled those things
of heaven and earth I'd never dreamed.
O mortal Prince of Denmark,
I, too, am human. Who is not passion's slave?
Who would want to live to tell,
sole survivor, ever marked by whispers
that trailed his dark-cloaked name?

James Scruton

Winter Forecast

Ignore all woolly worms, she said,
forget how many fogs before
the end of August, and instead
cut to the center of a fresh persimmon,
a dark fork at its core to show
the icy months ahead,
a spoon-shaped stain for snow.

Who would want to doubt it, to disbelieve
even so small a heart? Better
this afternoon to slice a persimmon
through the middle, wipe the knife clean
just above my shirt cuff, wear
the coming weather on my sleeve.

Something She Said

"Between Mars and California
there is a little patch of Tennessee,"
my friend the scientist told me,
referring, I would guess, to the bit
of everything out there, disunited states
of matter, whole galaxies
now ashes, dust to cosmic dust.

From Tennessee to California
Mars is low and red these evenings,
the closest, I heard on the news,
it will be for another eighty years.
Stared at for long it seems to pulse.
I think of my friend's poetic heart,
the fine gleam of her mind, pieces
enough of the universe.

Vivian Shipley

Praying you are asleep,

armed with a pen to write down a recipe in case
you're not, I slide down the hall of Pinewood Manor,
chanting to myself: pretend to need ingredients, ask
if it was pecans or walnuts you used for jam cake icing.

Always moving, Grandma, now you're pasted on the bed
like your wallpaper with flowers fading into red blotches.
One hundred years in disappearing, skin rises in dry ridges,
and your bones are getting easier to see. It's flannel that keeps

sunlight from shining right through you. Masking pooled
urine, the antiseptic odor of old age sits between us. Go back!
Fry chicken, slice ham and green cabbage for slaw. Never
thinking like Uncle Lanny of so many crops to a field,

your vegetable garden was ploughed inward, edge
to center with furrows squaring off even while the earth
changed color under Snip and Nellie's feet. Hop,
then stoop, you told me. Plant cucumbers, yellow squash

next to tomatoes and peppers; save the corn for last;
keep leftover seeds you sort out in the cracked mason jars.
Hoping you will die soon, I shrink from your bedside
like I did from the scarecrow you hung on broom handles.

I don't want to finger you, smell you or hear you talk about
being a girl and riding to Oklahoma in covered wagons then
back again to Kentucky. Winding a procession of plains,
crossing over the Tennessee border, you sat right up on

the edge of the board seat, straining to see Howe Valley.
Even then you listened for a voice saying, *You have found
the promised land.* There was no signpost to guide you.
Grandma, I have no words and no map to give you now.

Our bodies, arms of a weathervane pointing north and south,

Connecticut and Tennessee, we walk Appomattox, Virginia,
peeling years that wallpaper our Vanderbilt days. Martha, we're
growing old; I wouldn't travel except to see you. I think of my face
and how it must look to you now, how my waist has thickened.

Getting off the plane in Nashville, I sucked in but had to sag
back into myself. We repeat names as if fingering beads: Bill,
Cliff, Jimbo, Harry, Anne and Jennalie. I want to float out
over the corpse of my body while Cliff forgets the cigarette

he holds as he dances with me. How beautiful was the life of
the man we wanted to be: Dr. Duncan, fishing through coffee
money in Old Central, unsure of how many nickels he had put
in the plate. A cup, we can pass him between us like our notes

on Ruskin and Morris that we shared in his Victorian seminar that
first fall at Vanderbilt. Pausing at the ice house, we overlook what
might have been a point in the river where soldiers could cross
for breath in the wood. Death has cored this place like the hole

that held ice in walls of rough plank. There would have been
a pole with a hook that hung from a spike, a room where saws
were kept, a floor that stayed damp and cool. You explain
how ice was chunked and layered with straw to last the summer,

then pretend to be the cook who opened then quickly closed
the door to keep in winter. I picture us hanging up sere leaves
of lavender, lupine or Indian leaf from the overhang. It's quiet
now in McLean House, the doorway flanked with hollyhocks,

the rose and yellows contrasting their brave colors like the blue
and grey. In the photograph over an oval table with a marble top,
Grant and Lee are sitting right above where they must have been
sitting on April 9, 1865. They will sit forever posing between

two sets of curtains, now crimson velvet, that spill on the floor.
Like countless takes of Clark Gable and Vivien Leigh's farewell
Victor Fleming ordered in 1939 directing *Gone with the Wind*,
I add then cut detail after detail from scenes that might have been

acted on these fields. I create a starring role for myself: waking
the morning after a battle, I turn to cradle the head of my brother
in my hands, positioning them the way I did holding the bulb
of an amaryllis I had forgotten to take indoors after giving it

a day of sun in early spring. The temperature had dipped below
freezing that night. There was no resurrecting the plant or lives
left on these fields. What is left is memory of them like the white
bloom, bending into earth. Martha, we have awakened no rumble

of cannon. When a guard's not looking, we can stroke flow-blue
dishes. As if each meal was the source that renewed his passion,
General Lee wouldn't eat without them. The taste of dust rising
stays in our mouths. We've let our bodies go, let more than years

lapse. Resolving to go an a fat-free diet, meet next year at a spa.
I draw the line at liposuction, doing our eyes. Laughing at our hips,
our thighs, magic between us returns, and if we could only linger,
The Lady of Shallot might drift by. Nothing happens, but moving

of shadow across quiet water and stirring of heavy headed iris
so bronze and so big, they might be lanterns. As if we're playing
Tennyson for a seminar, we repeat, *She has a lovely face. / God
in his mercy lend her grace.* Subdued like the green by stillness,

we listen as a rising wind predicts autumn to the leaves that must
know what is forming in trees, just as the Confederates had to
suspect that Union troops were over the rise. Now, as soldiers
must have the last day, we listen for a voice to say, *Surrender.*

Arthur Smith

Paradise

I used to live there, I was born there, every morning
The downtown streets were cobbled with gold, honey
Flowed—all that stuff. I'm not kidding. Summers
Lasted a lifetime, broken by Christmas
And New Year's.
Mornings, like waking to someone's scent
You hadn't yet met and married for life,
Though I didn't know that then—the night-cooled
Muskmelons rolling belly-up to the stars,
And by late afternoon the dusk-colored
Dust of apricots on everything.
From that earth, my body
Assembled itself, and when the veil dropped,
I tried to say what I saw. The light winds
Around me died, the sheers of summer wavered
As though all of it were mirage. Cantaloupes,
Grapes, clusters of ruby flames, like champagne,
Though I didn't know that then—
Nectarines like morphine, nor that.
Oranges, almonds, rainbows,
Tangs—rolling in all year long, that bounty.
You tell people that, over and over,
And it's really crazy, they won't believe you.
All that sugar coaxed out of clay and you
Can't even give it away—and each dawn more
Was just piled on. I took in as much
As I could, like larder, and walked away.

Every Night as I Prayed God Would Kill You

Every night as I prayed God would kill you
In my heart, and every morning
The moment I awoke,
And all the day between,
For twelve months, one full year, I ached for you,
And then it stopped.

Not, of course,
All at once, and not as though, overnight,
The weeping willow bleeding leaves
Near the bedroom window
Were more vibrant, or the scent of hyacinths
Bunched in the planter
More coy than cloying.

The Tennessee did not surrender
Its river of coins, though it seemed
The morning light, rising, rocked on them,
Firing everywhere at once.

Nor did the animals approach me,
Heads lowered, with their solace.

Almost daily I walked the river bank,
Up and back, facing
The stark bluffs on the south shore
Where you lived,
And, one by one, I must have thrown
Half the pebbles
On the north shore into the middle.

The river pleased me, somehow—
The shore water simmered by fry and, farther out,
Small mouth churning the surface,
And powerboats plowing, and driftwood—
Bony knees knocking in the cove—
Gone the next day when I returned—
Come and gone
And coming around again
Like everything else,
With all the glitter and dazzle
And tedium and triviality, the hoopla and shouting,

And all the waste, especially the waste,
From which beauty wells.

That's when
It stopped enough for me to see
The tree leaves bathed in light,
And the feisty bluegill butting heads,
And, like plucked strings, the sprung cattails
Thrumming in the river's wash,
And a variable wind, and, over it all,
A fine mist that both soothes
And, bit by bit, erodes—small comfort,
This cooling off, this bearing down,
This wearing away.

More Lines on a Shield Abandoned During Battle

The one time I said something
Awful to someone
I didn't know the meaning of,
It hardly mattered to him how empty
My head was
As his three younger brothers jumped
Down from the barn loft they slept in
And closed ranks behind him.

The hen he'd been about to kill
Rejoined a few others feeding
Near the stump.

—Are you talking to me? he said.

And it's true—
As you and anyone who's ever scattered knows,
And usually sooner—someone or something
Will ask what you mean—
The quicker
The world lives in a person,
The earlier he learns
To ask.

I'm trying
To imagine racing over
Someone's countryside, and making off with its riches—
As you and your brief nation did—
Then coming up
Face to face
With one of them better armed.

I'm glad we ran, both of us, having
Straddled that line
Beyond which
There are only dogs' jaws
Candid
About the river of death,
And how there are no limits to its length,
And how someone had better live
To tell the others.

James Malone Smith

Mandelshtam's Wonderful Widow

—in memory of Donald Davie

The professor of Russian first.
Not a phonetic racket
or a scatter, as I expect,
but torsion—twists
of a screw into hard wood.
Then, lilting, by God.
Good humored, after all.

He bows to our translator
who recites, eyes closed
(as if Mandelshtam presides,
ear cocked). He alerts us to near
diffidence that may prevent
mishandling another's words,
as well as to necessary abandon . . .

More difficult than the Russian,
his poem has me fumbling
with words I comprehend.
Two rows down, a pony tail
jounces in approval,
her finger on a page following,
halting.

"Mandelshtam's wonderful widow . . ."
He prefaces the next poem,
but I do not yet know
(as the pony tail surely must)
about the smuggler's brilliance
of Nadezhda, and so conjure her
from a phrase.

                    Champagne glass aloft,
she stands in the midst of a party, silencing
the orchestra with a flick
of her hand. She delivers a toast
unintelligible to me
but to which the revelers
raise their glasses.

Steve Sparks

To Live Alone in Knoxville

In the concrete center of downtown
hunkers a commercial bakery
located across from a coffee
roasting house. First shifts
start at five. If the wind is right
(and it always is) the mixed aromas
of freshly baked bread and ground coffee
slink through your window, tuck
around you like an extra blanket,
and for the briefest moment,
you might think someone woke
before you and made breakfast.

David Stallings

Message

When I was small, I would leap
into the warm mitt of my father's lap
as he sat in his leather chair. Within his arms
I listened to Bible stories and fairy tales,
magically woke the next morning
in my bed.
After he died at 39,
my mother and uncles decided
I was too young to witness
his funeral.

In my fifties I find him—
buried beyond the Confederate section, under
the shady vase of an old elm.
He and a brother lie head to head, sharing opposite
sides of a six-foot block of polished granite.

I take my time with our meeting,
feel the warm day offer
a first breeze.
I place ocean stones upon his memorial,
weave soil from my Puget Sound home
into the land of his and my origin.
I glance the empty grounds,
            and lie atop
my father.

Close my eyes.

      A small insistence
on my left middle finger
calls me from dreamless sleep.
Through my half-opened left eye,
I watch a mockingbird
encode a long tattoo.

Humboldt, Tennessee, 1997

Darius Stewart

The Terribly Beautiful

To say this is the story of our lives.
Who is to say there is a story at all?
To be enchanted by a tune—
"Clair de Lune" from *Suite Bergamasque*—
when we complain moonlight pales
finer features of the disrobed body:
your sinewy muscles, my clumsy limbs.
To endure amaryllis blossoms season after season,
but the fly's life will last no longer
than the passing of one hour to the next.
To be the river that empties into the gulf,
& the gulf that destroys land
on which our houses are built.
To misunderstand the world we grieve.
To understand the grief.

Driftwood

The hours when the young sun grows old,
shade slants over the hibiscus leaves.
Jalal & I gather beneath porch-board
planks, sit hunched over. Down there
is a cavern, so black our skins glow
iridescent. Splinters hang like stalactites,
graze the curve of our spines.
We have done this every night, for so long—
Indian-style legs crush grass & weeds
pummeling through earth. We sit
hiding from the straight boys
moving above our heads, hear them whisper *where are they?*
They spread into the yard as though wolves
scavenging the plain, waiting as the sun slowly dies
behind the moon. No light will show our neon skins,
only their glowing, hollow eyes.
I arch my body over his, or his over mine,
& we take turns massaging the aches from our bodies.
When finally they return to the house,
the ear of the moon guides us from beneath the porch,
past the hibiscus, to the lake, where we sit
along the shore, watch small rippling tides.
We reach for driftwood, cast it back,
wish it was large enough to carry us.

Larry Thacker

Sing the Dead

I would sing the dead from the ground.
Stir them up clear from their dust,
coaxed high through the long six feet.
Who living recollects the songs of the dead?
How deeply the voice must echo,
how tightly to hug with a right vibration,
how close to their sleeping ears?

What is this obsession, this odd rehearsal,
not of death, but the full leading up to it?

In my dream my hands are gloved in mud,
boots sucked slurping down in the deep,
arms wrestling a shovel, slapping dark water
up out of the hole, a muddy cascade back
in my face, over and over, getting nowhere.
I've dug too deep. No voice yells the warning down.
I just feel it, as suddenly as the sun giving way to shadow.

What song lingers in the heavy absence of sun,
this hint of serenade lingering in the shadows?

In my dream I flee with smells of recent rain
and the dead's dust pressing damp the cloak
on my back and shoulders, weighting me down,
waiting down in the somewhere for me.

Have I retrieved that for which I searched,
between the mounds of fresh and dangerous earth?
So diligently between the towers of lightless stone?
So absent-heartedly between the memories
I've made up to fill in the gaps?

I think back at the many bodies I've seen.
Standing in polite lines, staring down on faces.
I can't see them without wondering—but don't we all
wonder how we'll look—lying there silk framed—

and wonder still on what we'll look like before
the mortician commences—as to what event
brings us merging arm in arm with such rest—
whether anyone might notice hints in our faces
as to what done us finally in—the dead talk,
and pray, and sing and commune. And having forever,
their whispered words nearly imperceptible,
take the rest of our lives to sing out the one word: live.

Kevin Thomason

Memphis

I've seen enough maps to know
how to make it back to Memphis.
As the crow flies, it's not far—

just miles and miles of air, Father,
but nothing's there I've left unfinished.
I've seen enough maps to know.

I never thought I'd follow
any road that led me into crisis,
but as the crow flies, it's never far.

I used to tell myself before,
that only miles and words were between us,
but now I've seen enough maps to know

there's nowhere that I could go
that I wouldn't simply think *this*,
as the crow flies, is not far

from Memphis, as I trace lines with my finger,
back bent, eyes squinted, judging distance.
I've seen maps enough to know,
as the crow flies, it's not far.

Susan O'Dell Underwood

For the Unwritten Hillbilly Poem

Raised on the King James Version,
how could they not love every storied word
of sacrifice and blood and bloom?
But they didn't have time,
not even for the hubris it would have taken,
to put beauty and anguish to rest
in their own words on the page.
The men worked along with the beasts in the field,
busting up stumps, hugging the boulders
of their destiny, no ownership except tomorrow.
The women, like Mary and Martha conjoined,
answered the needs of every crying, mewling thing,
every budding seed, watchful over the arrogant
demands of bubbling-up yeast dough.

Servants to duty, keepers of flame and smoke,
they built up to the ridge lines and then
over yonder, progeny rising up and West and gone,
toting the smoldering home-fire with them in metal buckets.
They stoked fires across two centuries,
leaving hardly a whisper, barely a signature,
no moment for anything except firing pits of charcoal,
brittle black of exodus and trade
that set this pig-iron country going;
no moment between designing the delicate scaffold
of kindling under the still
and setting fields of tobacco, cured
toward the promise of a well-earned smoke;
no moment between daylight's flicker of tinder
and the whole day's dark down in the mine;
no moment between cookstove dawn and hearth-fire night,
no moment between boiling the kettle for laundry
and stitching by kerosene lamp;
no moment except loading coal onto train cars
rolling in every direction like spokes on the wheel of genesis;
no moment to say rightfully what their lives were,
those rising up, lost sparks that started America.

Assimilation

Around here sometime not long ago,
we traded in lightning bug for the average firefly.
In the etymology of mountain entomology,
we've lost a few syllables here and there.
Why use three when two will do just fine?
That doesn't explain cicada, which we picked up
last time seventeen-year locusts came buzz-sawing around.
When we were kids, we all called them jarflies,
a poetic name enough for efficient double duty:
to name their havoc we swore
could shake black walnuts off the trees,
and describe as well as their amber shells,
replicating their poses like fragile, empty glass.

Some people don't like that bug's primeval rasp
any more than they abide a primitive tongue.
In college for a degree in communications,
they enrolled me in a voice and diction course
taught by Appalachian people
who had learned not to sound Appalachian.
I couldn't pronounce "i" to suit any ear
suited toward standard pronunciation,
and so I didn't earn the A,
held back by that letter of the alphabet
which stands for me, my consciousness, my ego and my id,
the one who must stand before God alone,
capitalized in English, a totem to explain the self.

The voice I hear recorded every now and then
I don't recognize as mine,
my dialect evolving toward the six o'clock news,
avoiding the slack, condescending mimicry
I might elicit, the dreaded open-mouthed gape
or worse, that coast-to-coast question, "Are you from Texas,"
and the worst-ever, "Where the hell are you from?"

Like a chameleon, which has four syllables,
I survive by being a difficult color to read,
code-shifting as fast as a NASCAR driver changes lanes.
But in my own, preferred slow element,
I think like a hellbender, that southern mountain lizard.
My accent when I talk to my mother, my father,

228

my family, finds me under a cool homey rock,
nowhere near the ire that drives us to be alike.
There I can hide from the bright shiny lights,
spiraling along the highways like sidewinding vipers,
the ones that threaten my demise.

Kory Wells

And This Will Be a Sign

To wake in this small room, where all night long
the steady furnace clicked and hummed soft warnings
to wolfish winds. To rise from quilted refuge,
don flannel robe and fur-lined slippers, pad
to chilly kitchen, brew the coffee, pour
the cream. To hold a cup that brims with comfort
and—dare you say it?—hope. As skeptics must,
you think this peace can't last, but how you wonder:

An old frame house. Thin walls and drafty sashes.
A Mason jar of holly twigs, a bauble
hanging here and there. Three presents wrapped
and waiting.
   Spare.
     Enough.
        For even now
your loved ones come this way, on frosty roads
in dazzling sun, their faces bright and open.

Daniel Westover

To a Tennessee Beech

Because you cannot be saved from the weight
of yourself, from a dry gut crossed by ant tunnels
or woodpeckers' persistent drills;
because yesterday my daughter pulled her blue wagon
through your shade; because even the living trees
are dropping leaves, and the coming snow
will sit heavy on sapless limbs; because you lean
leeward, threatening the deck like a prophecy;
you are coming down, and the back yard is a song
of chainsaws, of men shouting through your dust.

In the western desert, where I dragged grudging feet
behind my father, letting my spade scrape rocky ground,
trees grew reluctantly. Against wind he drove stakes,
lashed saplings to poles, corrected any slant.
Under his watch, I aimed strategic sprinklers,
painted the exposed trunks of plums,
sprayed peaches with sulfur and dormant oil,
troweled weeds from the base
of the one willow. In evening light we circled them,
my smaller shadow swallowed up in his.

Outside his shade, my feet no longer follow
across the yard, but there are days I think
I see him through the window, his loppers held out
like a divining rod, searching for something to remove,
something that's already gone. If he had been here
to see your ailing shape, to know your wrecked trunk
torn, pecked, hollowed and hived,
surely he would have done the same as I,
would have confessed that no surgical cut
or guy-rope's strain could keep you from falling.

Even so, to see you cut down here—my mountain home
where he has never been, where an unchecked
sprawl of gnarling oaks grows thick enough
to hide the neighbor's house—feels like failure;

231

and there is something in your ending,
played out against such excess of greenery,
that is cruel in its suddenness. Your lost shape
branches in me, and I know, remembering my father,
that there is no more time to take care,
that all the memory in the world cannot save us.

Waiting at the Crossing

After a photograph of my grandmother

From the platform, her thin body
leans forward, swept head to waist
with grainy light. Her daughter, not yet
my mother, will be on the evening train,
having dropped out of school
after less than a year. So she waits,
looks eastward, her hair riffling
in desert air, a black and white wind.

Still months away, her own train
comes into view, hums over a shale ballast
toward Mojave station and the choice
that will change her course like a switch
thrown down in a shunting yard,
taking her back to Appalachian hills.
Such green thoughts, still unnamed,
glow on sharp cheekbones, pull
her body from the platform shade.

I barely recognize the face, this woman
who cackles in our kitchen,
who smells like coffee and orange soap,
but she is no stranger. I watch her
not as myself, but with eyes borrowed
from a grandfather I never knew.
He holds the camera, watching
her body's slant, the way she leans
like potted orchids to a windowpane.

Years later, when he looked again
at this print worn smooth by his thumbs,
did he finally see the reason staring back?

Did he see it in the way she is looking
beyond Mojave, beyond the Air Force base
and Mustang football Friday nights,
to a life beyond the edges of his lens?

Or in that still moment,
did he know only the way this light
carries her; know only that the way
she is gazing down the sun-flared rails
made him want to capture her,
to hold her in the camera eye,
and frame the lonely radiance of her face?

Joe Wilkins

Ruins

The white line unravels, and I drive south
down Highway 51, a phantom road through levee
towns broke and open as half-hung
screen doors:
                    Wickliffe, Bardwell, Sassafrass Ridge—

here's the toothless maw of old downtown,
the bottle works a scrim of shattered glass,
                                                    derelict
tracks that cut the place in half, muddy-footed boys
tossing rocks at stumps.

                    ⟵

Last summer in Sunflower, Mississippi,
a black family rented a house across the tracks,
on the white side of town. My neighbors
said they were the first,
                            ever. Within a week
it burned to the foundation, the whole town
a hive of smoke.

                    ⟵

I've been lost three times since Chicago, since 6 AM
and my first plate of buttered grits in months—

                                            the South
begins somewhere outside Ashley, Illinois, where that two-lane
landed me in a cotton field, a cypress swamp, now the ruins

of Hickman, Kentucky.

                    ⟵

I teach 9th grade algebra in the little bayou town
of Indianola, Mississippi, and last year,
                                    the one-hundred

and thirty-third since Mississippi sent Hiram Revels
to the US Senate, the thirty-ninth since Fannie Lou Hamer
told the Democratic National Convention she was beaten

unconscious on the dirt floor of the Winona jail for trying
to register to vote, the ninth since the old-age death of the man
who hung a gin-fan around Emmet Till's neck and sunk him
in the Tallahatchie,
                              in the presidentiad of George W. Bush,
in the Year of our Lord 2003, out of the 156 children
that walked into my classroom every day, 154 were black—

all the white kids go to the academy across the tracks.

ෆ

Long haulers truck loads of toaster ovens
bound for the great,
                          glistening acres of box-stores
that ring Cordova, Tennessee. Tourists who can't find

the freeway drive for all their worth to get out quick.
Near the Hickman Liquor Mart, old men lounge
on hunks of levee stone.
                         I drive right through
the guts of town, but they eye me still
with indifference.

ෆ

It slides off your tongue like a goddamn snake—

Mississippi.

ෆ

The ancient river people hauled reed buckets
of black mud for temples the river always

                                 washed away.

Only dirt mounds are left, sudden domes
of kudzu and blackberry

and the far highway carrying me south.

ෆ

n. 1. *a cardinal point of the compass lying directly opposite*
north. 2. *the direction in which this point lies.*

$\qquad\qquad\qquad\qquad\qquad\qquad\qquad\qquad$ 3. *A region*

or territory situated in this direction. 4. *the general area south*
of Pennsylvania and the Ohio River
and east of the Mississippi,

$\qquad\qquad\qquad\qquad\qquad\qquad$ *consisting mainly*

of those states that formed the Confederacy.

*C*adj. 5. *lying toward or situated in the south;*
proceeding toward the south. 6. *coming from the south,*
as a wind.

$\qquad$ *C*adv. 7. *to, toward, or in the south.*
8. *into a state of serious decline, loss, or the like.*

$\qquad\qquad$ ☙

Once, on hall duty at Cassie Pennington Junior High,
I watched the school principal chase down a boy,
tackle him, and beat him with his fists.

The boy's name was Jermaine. He was fifteen
and read at a 2nd grade level. Two months later Jermaine
broke another boy's jaw.

$\qquad\qquad\qquad\qquad$ That boy sat in the front row

of my 7th period class, his smooth face swollen and bent,
and refused to do his work.

$\qquad\qquad$ ☙

But this morning
$\qquad\qquad$ the half-light lit the fields

like fire—cotton bolls gone red
and gold, the paper leaves of corn, soybeans
shining with something deep inside.

$\qquad\qquad\qquad\qquad\qquad$ And now,

as the sun escapes, the world goes water dark
and in the trees the soft slap of wind rises.

$\qquad\qquad$ ☙

I'm less than six hours out. I'm going back to Mississippi,
but I'm talking about America here

                                   the rot-wood
of The River Hotel in Cairo, shotgun shacks set back
in the trees,
               or a street in south Memphis, blue neon
hissing, rage of a cigarette, the warehouse door
banging on its hinge.

Outside a Liquor Store in South Memphis

To make a meal
of moths,

                   of mayflies—
black rag
of bat

              flaps in and out
of a streetlight's
incandescent stammer.

The dumb

        moon roped
and hung from eave
after rusted eave

                  of the empty
warehouses north of Raines.

And this neon

           sermon
of blue Camels, High Life,
Thunderbird—

                   such bright
appetites in the city's itching dark.

Rain Ghazal

We drive south out of Memphis, dark shoulders of rain
behind us. Now we turn west, towards the river, into rain.

The setting sun tumbles like a drunk through the trees,
and an old man fishing the bank lifts his face to rain.

I sit on the porch, sip whiskey from a jam jar, listen
for tree frogs and cicadas, for the lick of wind through rain.

Church Street is flooded. Don't try to drive it—it'll knock
your spark out. Road of dirty water, outrage of rain.

It comes down like rusty buckets, stumps, bricks. In the morning,
she lifts herself from the dark water of dreams, but still it rains.

Wind shakes pecans from the dark trees. Before dawn,
we wake and gather them in the fog, a gray wool of rain.

The soybeans drowned. The wheat rotted at the roots.
But green stalks swell between the dikes: rice loves rain.

A man holds a sopping bag over his head. Near the bayou,
a boy pulls off his shoes, his shirt, runs lazy eights of rain.

They wake in the dark, the heat of their sleep between them.
She swings her hips over his with the clatter of rain.

The road's a sudden river, trees thunder with dripping,
the sky no longer belongs to itself. All the world is rain.

Claude Wilkinson

Parable, Late October

Sunny undulations of butterflies all along I-40
        outside Jackson, Tennessee,
fluttered above, at times in front of noon traffic.

      Belched from
the stripped stalks of truck farms,
        metamorphoses rose

and dipped, sylphidine, through bell-clear air
        toward their new Canaan
of flowers. Every few hundred yards, they arced

        eighteen-wheelers,
salesmen chasing quotas, and me dodging
        the gossamer wings,

as if I were in harmony with sawing fiddlers
        on a bluegrass station
I'd picked up between towns, headed for the hospital

        in Memphis again
where my mother lolled on painkillers,
        had gone weeks

without solid food. Empty myself, unable to hold
        a night's thin soup,
I thought of Thanksgiving and Christmas approaching,

        our two times of indulgence,
remembered how even in years as lean as bone,
        she adorned our table

from dented tins marked "Crisco" and "flour,"
        from a full day spent
seasoning maw, whatever collards we'd gleaned

before caterpillars and frost.
You wonder, don't you, if there could ever be
perfect joy in anything

this fragile, always straddling benevolence?
Then, as if blood rain,
her life flooded over me, the way in autumn,

she'd sit on the porch
and watch our garden unscroll in a flourish
of yellow,

and with solemn disgust tell us,
"Them o butterflies
done ruined the little greens," just as one,

the color of fool's gold,
failed like stuttered prayer—a thumbnail flick
against my windshield,

sublime blossom of crimson, violet and bronze,
resplendent paradigm
revealing what the kingdom of heaven is like.

Sylvia Woods

Knowing

A child of Depression, blue-veined hands
map a life drawn from hilly acres, hands that
suckered tobacco, weeded corn, dug potatoes, endured
loss of child and man, palms open to help neighbors, kin.
On her front porch, she leans forward in painted chair,
breaks the tip of a half-runner, tugs string
down its spine. The pile grows like green spaghetti.
"Did you know the Chinese stir-fry green beans?"
asks a niece, the one who went to Europe junior year.
"And the French cut them slantwise with a knife."
"I simmer beans with a little fatback,
cook them hours, steam up the windows,
bake cornbread hot and crusty in the skillet
Mama left me." Mae says, "That is what I know."

Marianne Worthington

1116 N. 3rd Avenue, Knoxville, TN

He had not lived with her for sixty years
but her address emerged from his tangled
atlas of neurons. He shouted it with
confidence during the cognitive tests,
the only thing he'd said in days that made
much sense, even though her street was long
buried beneath the freeway, and her house
was as wrecked as his broken-down brain cells.

Surely her windows alight at Christmas
had sparked this synapse, the sheen on her stairs
inside the door, the little table-top
tree draped with ribbons, berries, and popcorn,
the curtains drawn back, a fire ablaze
in the grate, the damper wide open.

Paralysis

In my dreams my parents can always walk
unattended. No wheelchairs banging into walls,
no dead legs heavier than the weight of the world.

My father takes an incline at a trot. He is on a mission
to fix some widow woman's washing machine,
his toolbox swinging light as a dinner pail. The zeal
of his stride reminds me it's a dream, just a reverie.

My mother dances between the sewing notions
on her dining room table, Ray Charles on the stereo,
unbolts layers of creamy taffeta across the living
room floor, stumps on her knees to pin the pattern,
cuts, sews, finishes a bridesmaid's dress in an afternoon.

In the evening my father climbs the ladder to the attic
while my mother below wrestles Aunt Ala's old walker
to hoist up to him. He stores it between the joists,
caged protector held in the darkness to keep just in case.

Amy Wright

The Live Wires Tremble

for Kate Glasgow

A poem is not a lapdog, won't
come when you whistle,
waddling, eager to please. No. A poem is
a temptress & a vicar, a bit of threaded sand
woven by a heated spider, her belly an oven
of roiling emotional happening. Please
don't think you can tame anything
free and given. You've got to make yourself
a shimmering plate of composition, hold
your head tilted over the velvet keypad,
the mirrored reflection. There is no formula
but desire and patience, longing and fulfillment.
When she comes to you, honor her not
with clinging nor that spirit of ownership
you would no sooner use to degrade your lovers
whose very grace is dependent
not on what you command but how
you employ the pressure of exuberance.
You have your whole life
to visit every art museum, taste
each coconut gelato, thread each slip of yourself
into language. Be insistent. Know the muse
is more like a bad boy than a woman.
You can't woo him or demand anything,
but when he comes, hip cocked and lips soft
as the hearts he's broken, embrace the fact
that you want him. It is your strongest ally—
simplicity and the insatiable ache of vacancy.
The page fills like a heart that can never get enough
filling. Ask any rock star how it wants
to be loved.

Tornado Warning

A siren insists brusquely for us to "take shelter
immediately," at which point, various civilians
make their way to a windowless first floor copy room
where they talk casually about knee surgery
while drinking coffee & joking about bomb shelters
and food rations & someone muses what it would be like,
if you could—you know—safely, watch a funnel
touch down, which is happening
the next town over though no one's going to chase it,
& no doubt this conversation mirrors
a thousand others similarly wasted in moments
of human closeness in which no one confesses how much
they hunger and are hurt daily, as if a great wind
has already sucked them up from the center, whirled
them into an infinite vacuum of aloneness
if they can bear to be so very much together
& separate

Charles Wright

History Is a Burning Chariot

It is a good looking evening, stomped and chained.
The clouds sit like majesties in their blue chairs,
                                    as though doing their nails.
The creek, tripartite and unreserved, sniddles along
Under its bald and blow-down bridges.
It is a grace to be a watcher on such a scene.
So balance me with these words—
Have I said them before, I have,
                        have I said them the same way, I have
Will you say them again, who knows
                        what darkness snips at our hearts.

I've done the full moon, I've done the half moon and the quarter moon.
I've even done the Patrick Spens moon
As seen by one of his drowned sailors.
Tonight is the full moon again, and I won't watch it.
These things have a starting place, and they have an ending.
Render the balance, Lord,
                        send it back up to the beginning.

Lullaby

I've said what I had to say
As melodiously as it was given to me.

I've said what I had to say
As far down as I could go.

                                 I've been everywhere

I've wanted to but Jerusalem,
Which doesn't exist, so I guess it's time to depart,

Time to go,
Time to meet those you've never met,

                                             time to say goodnight.

Grant us silence, grant us no reply,
Grant us shadows and their cohorts

                                        stealth across the sky.

"What Becomes of the Broken Hearted . . ."

Up where the narrow bodies lie, suffused in sundown,
The children of God are stretched out

under the mountain,
Halfway up which the holy city stands, lights darkened.
Above the city, the nimbus of nowhere nods and retracts.

How is it that everyone seems to want

either one or the other?
Down here the birds leap like little chipmunks out of the long grasses.
Wind piddles about, and "God knows" is the difficult answer.

The children of Heaven, snug in their tiny pockets,
Asleep, cold,
Under the Purgatorial hill.
Soon they'll awake and find their allotted track

up to the upside down.

Or not. The gravetree estuaries against the winds of Paradise.
Unutterable names are unpinned from its branches.

A couple
Float down to this pocket, and others float down to that pocket.
Star shadow settles upon them,

the star shine so far away.

"Things Have Ends and Beginnings"

Cloud mountains rise over mountain range.
Silence and quietness,

sky bright as water, sky bright as lake water.
Grace is the instinct for knowing when to stop. And where.

Brenda Yates

Tennessee Jukebox

At the lunch counter in the retro-diner,
I punch E3, J2, K6, and order a hamburger,
shake, and fries. They're almost as good
as those first ones after three years
overseas, when we crossed the country
on two-lane blacktop and pulled into gravel
parking lots under neon "Eats."

Two stools down, an older man calls
the waitress over, says his coffee's
kindly cold. I don't hear the rest—
that intensifier jars loose something
lost for years: kindly aggravated
instead of pissed off or wicked mad.
Good ol' boys, young or old, trusted
and kindly close, who felt free to drop
in at supper time for soup beans
and corn bread at the kitchen table.
Where kindly slow meant that the child
in the adult's body who mowed your lawn
was to be spoken to with a gentle firmness
and kindly feeble was soon to die.

I start up a conversation with the man
just to listen to that old music,
then name my mother's small town.
Why, I's born 'n raised not
75 mile from there.
Before I can shake the drawl
from my voice, it comes out:
Yes, I kindly figured that.

Ray Zimmerman

Glen Falls Trail

I climb the limestone stairs
through an arch in rock,
into the earth's womb,
pass through to a surprise:
George loves Lisa painted on a wall.

I wonder, did he ever tell her?
Did she ever know or think of him,
raise a brood of screaming children?
Did they kiss near wild ginger
above the stony apse?

Did Lady's-slipper orchids
adorn their meeting place
where deer drink from rocky cisterns?
Did their love wither
like maidenhair fern,
delicate as English lace?

The symbols have outlived the moment.
There is only today, only
the murmur of water underground,
my finding one trickle into a pool.
I never knew this George or Lisa.
The rock bears their names in silence,
names the stream forgot long ago.

THE
POETS

DARNELL ARNOULT is Writer-in-Residence at Lincoln Memorial University in Harrogate, Tennessee. Her work has appeared in *Nantahala Review, Southern Cultures, Southwest Review, Southern Exposure, Asheville Poetry Review, Sandhills Review, Brightleaf, Now and Then Magazine,* and *Appalachian Heritage.* Her poems have been featured by Garrison Keillor on American Public Radio's *Writer's Almanac.* Her collection *What Travels With Us: Poems* (LSU Press) received the Weatherford Award for Appalachian Literature and the Southern Independent Booksellers Alliance Poetry Book of the Year. Her novel *Sufficient Grace* (Free Press) received a starred review from *Publisher's Weekly.* Arnoult is a recipient of the Mary Frances Hobson Medal for Arts and Letters and in 2007 was named Tennessee Writer of the Year by the Tennessee Writers Alliance. She holds an MFA from the University of Memphis and an MA from North Carolina State University.

BETH BACHMANN's first book, *Temper,* won the AWP Donald Hall prize and Kate Tufts Discovery Award and was published by the Pitt Poetry Series in 2009. Her new manuscript, *Do Not Rise,* was recently selected by Elizabeth Willis for the Poetry Society of America's Alice Fay di Castagnola Award for a manuscript in progress. She teaches at Vanderbilt University in Nashville, Tennessee.

JEFF BAKER grew up in East Tennessee near the birthplace of the Cherokee genius Sequoyah. His writing has benefited greatly from the insights of brilliant friends and mentors at both Tennessee Tech and the Iowa Writers' Workshop. Some of his recent poems have appeared, or are forthcoming, in *Blackbird, Boxcar Poetry Review, The Cream City Review, Copper Nickel, and Washington Square.* Jeff's work has been a finalist for numerous book prizes, including the *Bakeless Prize* and the *National Poetry Series.* He now lives and works in Charlottesville, Virginia.

EVELYN MCAMIS BALES, a native of Kingsport, Tennessee, has been published in *Appalachian Heritage, Bloodroot, Crossing Troublesome: Twenty-five Years of the Appalachian Writers Workshop, The Tennessee Sampler, Quill and Parchment,* and other journals and anthologies throughout the Appalachian region and beyond. Her poems were performed in Florida as part of *Tapestry,* a play by the Palm Beach Repertory Theater. Her chapbook *Kinkeeper* was published by *Finishing Line Press* as Number 18 in the New Women's Voices Series.

K. B. BALLENTINE received her MFA in Poetry from Lesley University, Cambridge, MA. She has participated in writing academies in both America and Britain and holds graduate and undergraduate degrees in English. She currently teaches high school theatre and creative writing and adjuncts for two local colleges. She has also conducted writing workshops throughout the United States. The 2013 Blue Light Press Book Award winner, K. B.'s third collection *What Comes of Waiting* is now available. Published in many print and online journals, KB has two collections of poetry: *Fragments of Light* (2009) and *Gathering Stones* (2008), published by Celtic Cat Publishing. In 2011, two anthologies published her work: *Southern Light: Twelve Contemporary Southern Poets* and *A Tapestry of Voices.* A finalist for the 2006 Joy Harjo Poetry Award and a 2007 finalist for the Ruth Stone Prize in Poetry, K. B. also received the Dorothy Sargent Rosenberg Memorial Fund Award in 2006 and 2007. Learn more about K. B. Ballentine at www.kbballentine.com.

COLEMAN BARKS was born in Chattanooga in 1937. He is best known for his collaboration with various scholars of the Persian language (most notably, John Moyne) to translate into American free verse the poetry of the 13th Century mystic, Jelaluddin Rumi.

This work has resulted in twenty-one volumes, including the bestselling *Essential Rumi* in 1995, and most recently, *Rumi: The Big Red Book* (2010), both from HarperOne. He has also published eight volumes of his own poetry, including *Winter Sky: New and Selected Poems, 1968-2008* and *Hummingbird Sleep, Poems 2009-2011* from the University of Georgia Press. In March 2005 the US State Dept. sent him to Afghanistan as the first visiting speaker there in twenty-five years. In May of 2006 he was awarded an honorary doctorate by the University of Tehran. He is now retired Professor Emeritus at the University of Georgia in Athens. He has two grown sons and five grandchildren, all of who live near him in Athens, Georgia. Website: colemanbarks.com.

TINA BARR's book, *The Gathering Eye*, won the Tupelo Press Editor's Award. She has received fellowships from the National Endowment for the Arts, the Tennessee Arts Commission, the Pennsylvania Council on the Arts, the MacDowell Colony, the Virginia Center for the Creative Arts, the Ucross Foundation, the Ragdale Foundation, and elsewhere. Her poems have been most recently published in *Shenandoah, The Antioch Review, Witness, Notre Dame Review, Mississippi Review, Brilliant Corners, Parthenon West Review, New South* and elsewhere, as well as in anthologies. She has published three chapbooks, *At Dusk on Naskeag Point*, (Flume Press, 1984) *The Fugitive Eye* (selected by Yusef Komunyakaa, Painted Bride Quarterly Press, 1997) and *Red Land, Black Land*, (Longleaf Press, Methodist College, Fayetteville, NC 2002).

JOHN BENSKO's books of poetry include *Green Soldiers* (Yale University Press), *The Waterman's Children* (University of Massachusetts Press), and *The Iron City* (University of Illinois Press). He also has a story collection, *Sea Dogs*, from Graywolf Press. He teaches in the MFA program at the University of Memphis and teaches a summer writing course in Spain, where he held a Fulbright Lectureship at the University of Alicante.

PETER BERGQUIST earned a BA in English from Princeton University and an MFA in Creative Writing from Antioch University Los Angeles. His poems have been published in *Rougarou, The Queen City Review, The New Verse News, A Handful of Dust* and *Broad River Review* among others. His poems "Gristle on the Bone," "The Easy Winter" and "Pulled Over Outside Santa Fe" were finalists for the latter journal's Rash Awards.

DIANN BLAKELY's third collection, *Cities of Flesh and the Dead*, won the Poetry Society of America's Alice Fay Di Castagnola Award, and she has appeared in numerous anthologies, including *Best American Poetry* and two volumes of *Pushcart*. Poems from her latest manuscripts—*Rain in Our Door: Duets with Robert Johnson* and *Lost Addresses*—have been featured twice in Greil Marcus's "Hard Rock Top Ten," as well as *New World Writing* and Lisa Russ Spaar's *Chronicle of Higher Education* poetry column. Blakely has been also published at *Harvard Review Online, The Nation, The Oxford American, The Paris Review, Parnassus, Triquarterly, Shenandoah, The Southern Review,* and *Verse,* among others, with recent prose contributed to *Antioch Review*, the *Best American Poetry* site, *Pleiades*, and *Smartish Pace*. She serves on the board of the transatlantic online journal *Plath Profiles* and has just been appointed a poetry editor at *New World Writing.*

LESLIE D. BOHN holds an MA from the University of South Dakota. Her poems have appeared in print and online journals such as *Ruminate, Relief, The Maynard,* and in *Poems & Plays* as a finalist for the Tennessee Chapbook Prize. She will always think of Nashville as home, but now resides in Cookeville, Tennessee with her husband who is a professor at the local university and her two-year old son who must think he is a muralist. When not writing or scrubbing paint from the walls, she is reading or running.

GAYLORD BREWER is a professor at Middle Tennessee State University, where he founded and for twenty years has edited the journal *Poems & Plays*. In May-June 2013 he was in residence at ARTErra in Portugal. His forthcoming ninth book of poetry is *Countries of Ghost* (Red Hen, 2015).

BILL BROWN is the author of three chapbooks, five collections of poetry, and a textbook. His most recent titles are *The News Inside* (Iris Press, 2010), *Late Winter* (Iris Press, 2008) and *Tatters* (March Street Press, 2007). In 1999 Brown wrote and co-produced the Instructional Television Series, *Student Centered Learning*, for Nashville Public Television. The National Foundation for Advancement in the Arts awarded him The Distinguished Teacher in the Arts. He has been a Scholar in Poetry at the Bread Loaf Writers Conference, a Fellow at the Virginia Center for the Creative Arts, and a two-time recipient of Fellowships in poetry from the Tennessee Arts Commission. The Tennessee Writers Alliance awarded Brown the 2011 Writer of the Year. He lives with his wife, Suzanne, and a tribe of cats in the hills north of Nashville.

KEVIN BROWN is an Associate Professor at Lee University and an MFA student at Murray State University. His poems have appeared or are forthcoming in *The New York Quarterly, REAL: Regarding Arts and Letters, Folio, Connecticut Review, South Carolina Review, Stickman Review, Atlanta Review,* and *Palimpsest,* among other journals. He has also published essays in *The Chronicle of Higher Education, Academe, InsideHigherEd.com, The Teaching Professor,* and *Eclectica.* He has one book of poetry, *Exit Lines* (Plain View Press, 2009), a chapbook, *Abecedarium* (Finishing Line Press), and a forthcoming book of scholarship: *They Love to Tell the Stories: Five Contemporary Novelists Take on the Gospels.*

DEVAN BURTON divides his time between Knoxville and Johnson City, Tennessee, and has written poetry for years. However, it was not until he took an American literature course at Roane State Community College that he realized the power of literature.

THOMAS BURTON was born in 1935 in Memphis, Tennessee, and received a PhD from Vanderbilt University in 1966. Burton is Professor Emeritus and was a member of the East Tennessee State University Department of English from 1958-1995. Burton is a collector of Appalachian culture and a documentary film maker. His most recent publication is *Beech Mountain Man: The Memoirs of Ronda Lee Hicks* (The University of Tennesseee Press, 2009).

MELISSA CANNON, born in New Hampshire in 1946, grew up in Tennessee. Educated at Swarthmore College and the University of Pennsylvania, she taught college English for ten years. Her work has appeared in many small-press journals and anthologies, including *HomeWorks* and *HomeWords,* two volumes by Tennessee writers published by the University of Tennessee Press. Her most recent publications include poems in *The Lyric, Ship of Fools,* and *Post Poems.* She lives in Nashville, retired after working in the fast-food industry for over twenty years.

CHRIS CEFALU's fiction, poetry, and essays have appeared in a wide variety of publications, including *Boulevard, The New York Quarterly* and *The Chariton Review.*

JAMES E. CHERRY's latest collection of poetry, *Loose Change,* was published in the spring of 2013 from Stephen F Austin State University Press. His previous volume of verse, *Honoring the Ancestors,* (Third World Press) was nominated for an NAACP Image Award. A fiction writer as well, he lives in Tennessee with his wife and is preparing a novel for publication. He is available on the web at http://www.jamesEcherry.com.

CATHERINE PRITCHARD CHILDRESS lives in the shadow of Roan Mountain, Tennessee. She received her MA in English from East Tennessee State University, where she served as editor of *The Mockingbird* Literary/Arts journal. Her poems have appeared or are forthcoming in *North American Review, The Connecticut Review, Louisiana Literature, Cape Rock, Still: The Journal,* and *Southern Women's Review* among other journals.

KEVIN MARSHALL CHOPSON received his MFA from Murray State University in Kentucky. His work has been published in *English Journal, The South Carolina Review, REAL: Regarding Arts and Letters, Concho River Review, The Chaffin Journal, The Aurorean, San Pedro River Review, Poem, National Gallery of Writing, Tipton Poetry Journal, Generations, Birmingham Arts Journal, Black Magnolias, The Broad River Review, Chiron Review, Tennessee English Journal, Nashville Arts Magazine, New Madrid, Number One, The Hurricane Review,* and *The Baltimore Review.* He teaches writing at Davidson Academy and Volunteer State Community College, both just north of Nashville, Tennessee. He hopes soon to find a publisher for his first collection, entitled "The Projector."

SAMUEL CHURCH moved to East Tennessee eleven years ago, after spending time in Kentucky and Mississippi. He received BA in English from East Tennessee State University and is currently enrolled at Milligan College in Johnson City, Tennessee. His poems have appeared in *Now and Then* and *A! Magazine for the Arts.*

GEORGE DAVID CLARK is currently the Olive B. O'Connor Fellow in Creative Writing at Colgate University. He holds an MFA from the University of Virginia and is a candidate for the PhD in Literature and Creative Writing at Texas Tech. His poems have most recently appeared in *The Journal, Shenandoah, Smartish Pace, Southern Poetry Review,* and *Willow Springs* and can be found online at *Verse Daily, Poetry Daily,* and *Linebreak.* He is the editor of *32 Poems Magazine* and lives with his wife and son in Earlville, New York.

JIM CLARK was born in Byrdstown, Tennessee, and educated at Vanderbilt University, the University of North Carolina at Greensboro, and the University of Denver. He is the Elizabeth H. Jordan Professor of Southern Literature and Chair of the Department of English, Modern Languages, Religion, and Philosophy at Barton College in Wilson, North Carolina. His books include *Notions: A Jim Clark Miscellany* and two collections of poetry, *Dancing on Canaan's Ruins* and *Handiwork;* he edited *Fable in the Blood: The Selected Poems of Byron Herbert Reece.* His work has appeared in *The Georgia Review, Prairie Schooner, Denver Quarterly, Greensboro Review,* and *Asheville Poetry Review.* He has released two solo CDs, *Buried Land* and *The Service of Song,* and three CDs with his band The Near Myths, *Wilson, Words to Burn,* and *. . . and into the flow.*

After growing up in the Carolinas, MICHAEL CODY spent his early adult life in Nashville, Tennessee, where he worked as a songwriter for several publishing companies and fronted a band that played original music. Following this, he returned to the mountains, married his seventh-grade sweetheart, and spent a decade in school—UNC-Asheville, Western Carolina

University and USC-Columbia. He teaches English at East Tennessee State University in Johnson City. His fiction and poetry have appeared in *The Howl, Pisgah Review, Short Story, Yemassee, Potpourri*, and *Fury*.

LISA COFFMAN is the author of two poetry collections, *Less Obvious Gods* and *Likely*. She has received fellowships for her poetry from the National Endowment for the Arts, the Pew Charitable Trusts, the Pennsylvania Council on the Arts, and Bucknell University's Stadler Center for Poetry. Her work has appeared in numerous literary magazines and anthologies, including *Myrrh, Mothwing, Smoke: Erotic Poems, Listen Here: Women Writing in Appalachia, A Fine Excess: Fifty Years of the Beloit Poetry Journal*, and *American Poetry: The Next Generation*. She was awarded the 2010 Ingrid Reti Nonfiction Prize for her work "No Business, Tennessee," about the 1933 Boyatt-Winningham tragedy on the Upper Cumberland Plateau.

ROBERT G. COWSER began writing poetry in the '70s, often focusing on the personal lyric and nature subjects. Many of his poems contain literary allusions. Cowser's son, Bob, Jr., edited a chapbook of his father's poems in 1990 (*Backtrailing*, The University of Tennessee at Martin). Cowser's most recent chapbook is *Selected Poems, 2nd Ed. 1985-2010* (The University of Tennessee at Martin, 2013).

THOMAS CROFTS teaches and writes his poetry in Johnson City, Tennessee, where he is associate professor in the Department of Literature and Language at East Tennessee State University. His poems have appeared in *The Texas Observer, Upstart Crow*, and *Born Magazine* as well as a few self-published chapbooks. He lives with Molly, Rex, Augie, and Shadow.

KATE DANIELS was educated at the University of Virginia (BA and MA in English Literature) and Columbia University (MFA, School of the Arts). Her teaching career has taken her to the University of Virginia, the University of Massachusetts at Amherst, Louisiana State University, Wake Forest University, Bennington College, and Vanderbilt University, where she is an associate professor of English and Chair of the Vanderbilt Visiting Writers Series. Her first book of poetry, *The White Wave* (Pittsburgh, 1984), won the Agnes Lynch Starrett Poetry Prize. Her second volume, *The Niobe Poems* (Pittsburgh, 1988), received honorable mention for the Paterson Poetry Prize. *Four Testimonies*, her third volume, was one of Dave Smith's selections for his Southern Messenger Series, published by LSU Press (1998). Her fourth volume is entitled *A Walk in Victoria's Secret*. Daniels was named the winner of the 2011 Hanes Award for Poetry by the Fellowship of Southern Writers for her work to date.

RYAN DIXON was born and raised in Chattanooga and attended the University of Tennessee at Chattanooga. For the past five years, he has taught American literature at an international school in Seoul, South Korea. It was after moving to Korea that his East Tennessee roots began to influence his writing. Currently, he teaches high school English in Memphis.

A recent graduate of the University of Tennessee, ENA DJORDJEVIC is a Serbo-Croatian refugee and current MFA candidate at the University of Maryland. Her work has appeared in *J Journal* and *The Smoking Poet* (online). She has been nominated for the AWP Intro Journals Project and has received University of Maryland's Academy of American Poets prize.

HEATHER DOBBINS's poems have appeared in *Big Muddy, Chiron Review*, and *TriQuarterly Review*, among others. She was the featured poet for *Beloit Poetry Journal* in June 2013. She writes poetry reviews for *The Rumpus*. After ten years of earning degrees in California and Vermont, she returned to her hometown of Memphis, where she is currently a writing instructor and college counselor at a special needs high school.

LISA DORDAL lives in Nashville, Tennessee, with her partner, Laurie, and their greyhound, Ladybug, and currently teaches part-time in the English Department at Vanderbilt University. Dordal's poetry has appeared in a variety of journals, including *Cave Wall, Sugar House, The Sow's Ear Poetry Review, Sinister Wisdom, Bridges: A Jewish Feminist Journal*, and *The Journal of Feminist Studies in Religion*, as well as in several anthologies, including *Milk and Honey: A Celebration of Jewish Lesbian Poetry* (A Midsummer Night's Press, 2011). Her chapbook, *Commemoration*, was released in 2012 by Finishing Line Press. For more information about her poetry, please visit her website at http://lisadordal.com.

DONNA DOYLE was born and raised in East Tennessee. Her poems have been published in several anthologies, including *The Southern Poetry Anthology, Volume III: Contemporary Appalachia*. Journal publications include CHEST, *Journal of the American Medical Association (JAMA), Now & Then*, and *Still*. She is the author of a chapbook, *Heading Home*, published by Finishing Line Press. Donna facilitates poetry workshops in healthcare settings and mentors health sciences students in the practice of narrative medicine. She is poet-in-residence at the University of Tennessee Graduate School of Medicine's Preston Medical Library, where she manages an author reading/conversation series, Literary Rounds: Where Medicine Mingles with the Muse. Related interviews have been featured in *Smoky Mountain Living* and *KnoxZine*. Donna's latest poetry project is *Random Acts of Haiku*—recently launched on Facebook. She lives in Knoxville, Tennessee.

JOHN DUCK earned an MFA from the University of Maryland. A graduate of the University of Tennessee, his work has appeared previously in *Kestrel* and *TheSmokingPoet.com*.

BENJAMIN DUGGER was born and raised in East Tennessee, where his ancestors settled in the 1760s. He holds degrees from East Tennessee State University, The Southern Baptist Theological Seminary, and George Mason University. He has taken post-graduate work at East Tennessee State University, the University of Maryland, and Wesley Theological Seminary (Washington, DC), and has studied abroad in England, Northern Ireland, and the School of Scottish Studies at the University of Edinburgh, Scotland. He also received training in Syro-Palestinian Archaeology at Tell Gezer, Israel, with the American Schools of Oriental Research in Jerusalem. His poems have been published in anthologies, arts magazines, newspapers, and on the Internet. His published photography has appeared in Scotland as well as the United States. He was a pastor for twenty-two years and is currently an associate portfolio manager with The Burney Company, an equity research and investment advisory firm headquartered in Falls Church, Virginia.

SUE WEAVER DUNLAP grew up in Knoxville, Tennessee, and now lives further back in the Smokies in Walland, Tennessee. She is a semi-retired high school English teacher and periodically adjuncts at Walters State Community College. Her work has appeared in *Appalachian Heritage, Outscape: Writing on Fences and Frontiers, Anthology of Appalachian Writers* (Volumes III, IV, & V), *Remember September*, and *Among These Hills*. When not writing or teaching, Sue enjoys hiking, reading, or generally just roaming the mountains she calls home. She and her husband Raymond raise Black Angus cattle and spend time just hanging out with their dog and cat, watching turkeys forage in their yard.

RENEE EMERSON earned her MFA in poetry from Boston University. Her first book of poetry, *Keeping Me Still* (Winter Goose Publishing, 2014) is forthcoming, and her poetry has been published in *32 Poems, Christianity and Literature, Indiana Review*, and elsewhere. Renee teaches at Shorter University in Rome, Georgia, where she lives in a little brick house in the woods with her husband and daughters.

BLAS FALCONER is the author of *The Foundling Wheel* and *A Question of Gravity and Light*. The recipient of an NEA Fellowship and the Maureen Egen Writers Exchange, he teaches creative writing in the low-residency MFA program at Murray State University.

MERRILL FARNSWORTH's collection of stories, *Jezebel's Got the Blues*, will be featured at Nashville's 25th Annual Southern Festival of Books (October 2013). Her poems and short stories can be found in *Silver: An Eclectic Anthology of Poems and Prose, Green: An Eclectic Anthology of Poetry and Prose*, and *Summer Anthology* (Silver Birch Press). Like everyone in Nashville, Farnsworth is a songwriter. She penned lyrics for the title cut of *Mercyland*, a project featuring Emmylou Harris, Phil Madeira, The Civil Wars, Carolina Chocolate Drops, North Mississippi Allstars, and other artists. Farnsworth, who believes every life has a story to tell, is the founder of writingcircle.org.

WILLIAM ROBERT FLOWERS was born and raised in Humboldt, Tennessee. He received his MFA from the University of North Carolina at Wilmington in 2010, and he currently works at the University of Tennessee at Martin. His poetry has been featured in journals such as *Hunger Mountain, Bellingham Review, Apple Valley Review*, and several others, as well as the recent anthology *A Face to Meet the Faces: A Contemporary Anthology of Persona Poetry*.

KITTY FORBES lives with her husband Walter and dog Yankee-Poodle in Lookout Mountain, Georgia, near Chattanooga. She graduated from the University of Georgia and received her MFA from Vermont College. She also studied with Richard Jackson at the University of Tennessee, Chattanooga. In August, she was a participant in the Sewanee Writers Conference, where she studied with Mary Jo Salter. Last winter she was awarded a residency at Virginia Center for the Creative Arts. Her poems appear in the *Atlanta Review, California Quarterly, Main Street Rag, The Oxford American, The MacGuffin*, and others. She loves to read, write, garden, and make music. She has appeared many times in local theater productions, and she sang with her husband on Nashville's *Grand Ol' Opry* and other musical venues.

LUCIA CORDELL GETSI has published five volumes, one a critical translation of the poems of Georg Trakl; hundreds of poems, fiction, translations, and critical, scholarly and personal essays; and has been awarded national and international prizes and fellowships, including the Capricorn Prize, two research Fulbrights, an NEA in Poetry, and five Illinois Arts Council Artist fellowships. She is Distinguished Professor Emerita of Illinois State University and twenty-year Editor Emerita of *The Spoon River Poetry Review*.

RON GILES, a retired English teacher, lives in Johnson City, Tennessee, with his wife, Gwendolyn. His poems have appeared, most recently, in *Silk Road, Paper Street,* and *The Alembic.* A one-act play, *Moses Otis Is Not a White Man,* received a staged reading at the Great Plains Theatre Conference (2007), in Omaha.

LEA GRAHAM is the author of a book of poems, *Hough & Helix & Where & Here & You, You, You* (No Tell Books, 2011) and a chapbook, *Calendar Girls* (above/ground Press, 2006). Her poems, translations, reviews, and essays have been published in places like *Notre Dame Review, The Southern Humanities Review, Fifth Wednesday,* and several anthologies. She was born in Memphis and grew up in Northwest Arkansas. She is currently Associate Professor of English at Marist College in Poughkeepsie, New York.

CAROL GRAMETBAUER writes poetry in Kingston, Tennessee. She is chairman of the board of directors of Tennessee Mountain Writers and had a twenty-five-year career in public relations. Her poems have appeared in *Appalachian Heritage, POEM, The Cabinet* (published by *Potomac Review*) and the online journals *Still: The Journal, drafthorse,* and *Maypop,* as well as in *Remember September: Prompted Poetry,* edited by Patricia Hope. Publication is pending in *The Kerf.*

JESSE GRAVES grew up in Sharps Chapel, Tennessee, the community his ancestors settled in the 1780s. He is an Assistant Professor of English at East Tennessee State University, where he was granted the 2012 New Faculty Award from the College of Arts & Sciences. Graves's first collection of poems, *Tennessee Landscape with Blighted Pine,* won the 2012 Weatherford Award in Poetry, and the Poetry Book of the Year Award from the Appalachian Writers' Association. His chapbook, *Basin Ghosts,* is forthcoming from Texas Review Press.

CONNIE JORDAN GREEN's two novels for young people, *The War at Home* and *Emmy,* were reissued in soft cover by Tellico Books, an imprint of Iris Publishing. Her two poetry chapbooks, *Slow Children Playing* and *Regret Comes to Tea,* are from Finishing Line Press. The novels' awards include listing in the American Library Association's Best Books for Young Adults and selection as a Notable Children's Trade Book in the Field of Social Studies. Her poetry has appeared in numerous publications, most recently *Appalachian Heritage, Crossroads, drafthorse, Now & Then, Potomac Review, STILL,* and anthologies *Outscape; Motif: Writing by Ear; The Southern Poetry Anthology, Volume III; Contemporary Appalachia; Anthology of Appalachian Writers Vol. V;* and *Poem in Your Pocket for Young Poets.* Since 1978 she has written a column for *The Loudon County News Herald.* She teaches creative writing and literature for Oak Ridge Institute of Continued Learning.

RASMA HAIDRI grew up in Tennessee with a Norwegian-American mother and South Asian father. She now lives on the arctic seacoast of Norway where she teaches English. Her writing has appeared in many literary magazines, including *Nimrod, Prairie Schooner, Kalliope,* and *Fourth Genre,* and has been widely anthologized from publishers such as Seal Press, Bluechrome, Puddinghouse, Marion Street Press, and Bayeux Arts. Among awards for her work are the Southern Women Writers Association Emerging-writer Award in creative non-fiction, the Mandy Poetry Prize, and the Wisconsin Academy of Arts, Letters & Science Poetry Award. She has received grants from Vermont Studio Center and the Norwegian Non-fiction Writers and Translators Association.

PATRICIA L. HAMILTON is Professor of English at Union University in Jackson, Tennessee, where she teaches 18th-century British literature and creative writing. She earned her PhD at the University of Georgia. Her most recent work has appeared in *Poetry South, Cumberland River Review, Iodine Poetry Journal, Sierra Nevada Review,* and *Plainsongs.* Her first volume of poetry, *The Distance to Nightfall,* is forthcoming from Main Street Rag Press.

JEFF HARDIN, originally from Savannah, Tennessee, is an eighth generation descendant of the founder of Hardin county. He holds degrees from Austin Peay State University and the University of Alabama. A professor of English at Columbia State Community College in Columbia, Tennessee, he is the author of two chapbooks and two collections: *Fall Sanctuary,* recipient of the 2004 Nicholas Roerich Prize, and *Notes for a Praise Book.* His poems have appeared in *The Southern Review, Hudson Review, Gettysburg Review, North American Review, Southwest Review, The New Republic, Poetry Northwest, Measure, Tar River Poetry, Meridian, Poet Lore,* and many others. His work has also been featured on *Verse Daily, Poetry Daily,* and Garrison Keillor's *The Writer's Almanac.*

KAY HECK is an Associate Professor of English at Walters State Community College where she teaches composition, literature, dual enrollment, and RODP courses. She grew up in historic Rogersville, the basis for most of her poetry and short stories. She received degrees from WSCC and East Tennessee State University. After college, she served several years with Amor Ministries, an urban/Mexican relief organization based in Fullerton, California, and also taught courses at Hope International University and Fullerton College. Upon returning to her beloved East Tennessee, she served as an Assistant Campus Minister with the Christian Student Fellowship at ETSU and also took graduate courses at Emmanuel School of Religion before returning to teaching. Her works have appeared in *Appalachian Journal, Outscape: Writing on Fences and Frontiers, Appalachian Literature and Culture Journal, Muscadine Lines, Perspectives,* and *The Encyclopedia of Appalachia.*

A native of upper East Tennessee, JANE HICKS is an award-winning poet and quilter. Her poetry appears in both journals and numerous anthologies, including *Southern Poetry Anthology, Volume III: Contemporary Appalachia.* Her first book, *Blood and Bone Remember,* was nominated for and won several awards. Her "literary quilts" illustrate the works of playwright Jo Carson and novelists Sharyn McCrumb and Silas House; one became the cover of her own book. The art quilts have toured with these respective authors and were the subject of a feature in *Blue Ridge Country Magazine* in an issue devoted to arts in the region. The University Press of Kentucky will publish her latest poetry book, *Driving with the Dead,* in 2014.

GRAHAM HILLARD is the founding editor of *The Cumberland River Review* and an associate professor of English at Trevecca Nazarene University in Nashville. His poems, essays, and stories have appeared in *The Journal, The Oxford American, Puerto del Sol, Regarding Arts and Letters, Tar River Poetry,* and many other magazines. His investigative feature "A Killing in Cordova: The Trial and Tribulations of Harry Ray Coleman" (*Memphis*) was a finalist for the 2012 Livingston Award for Young Journalists.

RICK HILLES is the author of *Brother Salvage,* winner of the 2005 Agnes Lynch Starrett Poetry Prize, also named the 2006 Poetry Book of the Year by *ForeWord Magazine* (now *ForeWord Reviews,* which celebrates independent and small press publishing), and *A Map of the Lost World* (2012), currently a finalist for the 2013 Ohioana Book Award, both with the University of Pittsburgh Press. He has been the recipient of a Whiting Writers' Award, the Amy Lowell Poetry Traveling Scholarship, a Camargo Fellowship, and, most recently, a 2013 Individual Artist Fellowship in Poetry from the Tennessee Arts Commission. His poems have appeared in *Poetry, The Nation, The New Republic, Paris Review, Ploughshares*, and *Salmagundi*. He lives in Nashville and is an assistant professor of English at Vanderbilt University.

ANGIE HOGAN's poems have appeared or are forthcoming *The Antioch Review, Notre Dame Review, Ploughshares, Poet Lore, Quarterly West, The Threepenny Review*, and *The Virginia Quarterly Review*, among other journals. She has also had work featured online at *Poetry Daily* and *From The Fishouse*. Hogan holds degrees from Vanderbilt University and The University of Virginia, where she was a Henry Hoyns Fellow. Additional honors include a Jacob K. Javits Fellowship and an Academy of American Poets Prize. Originally from a small town in East Tennessee, she now resides near Charlottesville and works at the University of Virginia Press.

THOMAS ALAN HOLMES, a member of the East Tennessee State University English faculty, lives and writes in Johnson City, Tennessee. Some of his work has appeared in *Louisiana Literature, Valparaiso Poetry Review, The Connecticut Review, The Appalachian Journal, Seminary Ridge Review, The Florida Review, Blue Mesa Review, The Black Warrior Review, Cape Rock Journal*, and *The Southern Poetry Anthology, Volume III: Contemporary Appalachia*.

SCOTT C. HOLSTAD is the poetry editor for *Ray's Road Review* and holds degrees from the University of Tennessee, California State University Long Beach, and Queens University of Charlotte. He has authored fifteen volumes of poetry. His work has appeared in hundreds of magazines worldwide, including *The Minnesota Review, Wisconsin Review, Hawaii Review, Chiron Review, Pearl, Atom Mind, Long Shot, Exquisite Corpse, Caffeine, Pacific Review, Palo Alto Review, Santa Clara Review, Poetry Ireland Review, Arkansas Review, Awakenings Review, Lullwater Review, Asheville Poetry Review*, and *Southern Review*. He lives in Chattanooga with his wife, Gretchen, and two spoiled cats.

HEATHER M. HOOVER earned her PhD in literature from the University of Tennessee in 2010 with a dissertation focus on poetry, theology, and ecocriticism. Currently, she is an Associate Professor of English and Composition and the George and Janet Arnold Chair of the Humanities at Milligan College in East Tennessee. She teaches 20th Century American literature, composition, and poetry in addition to directing the writing program.

JANICE HORNBURG is a native Texan who transplanted to East Tennessee in 1993. She earned a Bachelor's degree from Houston Baptist University in 1970, and is employed as a clinical research scientist involved in the FDA approval of new drugs. She is a member of the Poetry Society of Tennessee, the North Carolina Writers' Network, and the Lost State Writers' Guild. She has won numerous first-place awards for her poetry. Finishing Line Press released Janice's chapbook, *Perspectives*, in May 2013. Her work has appeared in the *Anthology of Appalachian Writers, Gretchen Moran Laskas, Volume V, Tennessee Voices, 2012-2013*, and *Chapter 16*.

ELIZABETH HOWARD lives in Crossville, Tennessee. Her work has appeared in *Comstock Review, Big Muddy, Appalachian Heritage, Cold Mountain Review, Poem, Motif, Mobius, Now & Then, Slant, Still*, and other journals.

DORY HUDSPETH grew up close to Springfield, Tennessee, and has crossed the border, now living in Alvaton, Kentucky. She is an herbalist, freelance writer, and poet. Her poems have appeared in *Rattle, Wavelength, Shenandoah, Sow's Ear Review, Slant, Runes, Atlanta Review* and other journals. Her first poetry collection is *Enduring Wonders* from WordTech Press, and her chapbook, *I'll Fly Away*, is from Finishing Line Press.

H. K. HUMMEL is a lecturer in the Department of Rhetoric and Writing at the University of Arkansas at Little Rock and editor of the literary journal *Blood Orange Review*. She has published two chapbooks, *Boytreebird* (2013) and *Handmade Boats* (2010), and her work has appeared in journals such as *Meridian, Sugar Mule, Poemeleon*, and *Antigonish Review*. She received the Katharine Susannah Prichard Emerging Writer-in-Residence award in 2009, and she holds an MA in English Literature from Eastern Washington University, and a BA in English from the University of California, Davis.

JANNETTE HYPES is a South Carolina native who became an East Tennessean in 1998. A graduate of USC-Aiken, where she studied poetry and life with Dr. Stephen Gardner, her poetry has appeared in *Breathing the Same Air: An East Tennessee Anthology* (Celtic Cat Publishing, 2001); *The Southern Poetry Anthology, Volume I: South Carolina* (Texas Review Press, 2007); *Outscapes: Writings on Fences and Frontiers* (Knoxville Writers' Guild, 2008); and *The Southern Poetry Anthology, Volume III: Contemporary Appalachia* (Texas Review Press, 2011).

RICHARD JACKSON has been awarded the Order of Freedom Medal by the President of Slovenia for literary and humanitarian work in the Balkans, he has been named a Guggenheim Fellow, Fulbright Fellow, Witter-Bynner Fellow, NEA fellow, NEH Fellow, and he has lectured and given readings at dozens of universities and conferences in the US and abroad. In 2009 he won the AWP George Garret National. He is the author of ten books of poems, including *Resonance* (2010) (Eric Hoffer Award), *Half Lives: Petrarchan Poems* (2004) and *Unauthorized Autobiography: New and Selected Poems* (2003). He has also published two books of translations, *Last Voyage: The Poems of Giovanni Pascoli from Italian* (2010) and Alexandar Persolja's *Journey of the Sun from Slovene* (2008). He is also the author of two critical books and has edited two anthologies of Slovene poetry, as well as the journal *Poetry Miscellany*. His work has been translated into fifteen languages. His eleventh book of poems, *Out of Place*, will appear in February of 2014.

MARK JARMAN has published ten volumes of poetry, including *Iris* (a book-length poem), *Questions for Ecclesiastes, To the Green Man*, and *Epistles* (a collection of prose poems). His new and selected poems, *Bone Fires*, was published in 2011 and won the 2011 Balcones Prize for poetry. Among his awards are a Guggenheim Fellowship, the Lenore Marshall/ *Nation* Prize of the Academy of American Poets, and The Poets' Prize. His poems have appeared in journals such as the *American Poetry Review, The New Yorker*, and *The Atlantic Monthly*. He is also the author of two collections of essays: *The Secret of Poetry* and *Body and Soul: Essays on Poetry*.

T. J. JARRETT is a writer and software developer in Nashville, Tennessee. Her recent work has been published or is forthcoming in *Boston Review, Beloit Poetry Journal, Callaloo, DIAGRAM, Ninth Letter, Rattle, Third Coast, West Branch*, and others. She has earned scholarships from the Sewanee Writer's Conference and Colrain Manuscript Conference. Her collections have been runners up for the 2012 Marsh Hawk Poetry Prize and 2012 New

Issues Poetry Prize, and a finalist for the 2010 Tampa Review Prize for Poetry. Her debut collection *Ain't No Grave* will be published with New Issues Press (Western Michigan). Her second collection, *Zion* (winner of the Crab Orchard Open Competition, 2013), will be published by Southern Illinois University Press in the fall of 2014.

DON JOHNSON is a professor and Poet in Residence at East Tennessee State University in Johnson City, Tennessee, where he has been a member of the faculty for thirty years. Johnson's poetry publications include: *The Importance of Visible Scars* (1984), *Watauga Drawdown* (1991), *Here and Gone: New and Selected Poems* (2010), and numerous publications in such journals as *Poetry*, *The Iowa Review*, *The Georgia Review*, and *Prairie Schooner*. He has also written extensively on the literature of sport and Appalachian literature. His fourth book of poems, *More than Heavy Rain*, will appear in Spring 2014 from Texas Review Press.

MARILYN KALLET is the author of sixteen books, including *The Love that Moves Me*, *Packing Light: New and Selected Poems*; *The Big Game*, translated from Benjamin Péret's *Le grand jeu*, and *Last Love Poems of Paul Eluard*, all from Black Widow Press. She directs the Creative Writing Program at the University of Tennessee, where she is Nancy Moore Goslee Professor of English. She also teaches poetry workshops for the Virginia Center for the Creative Arts, in Auvillar, France. She has won the Tennessee Arts Commission Literary Fellowship in Poetry, and she was inducted into the East Tennessee Literary Hall of Fame in 2005. Kallet has performed her poetry on campuses and in theaters across the United States, as well as in France and in Warsaw and Krakow, as a guest of the United States Embassy's "America Presents" program.

HELGA KIDDER has lived in the Tennessee hills for thirty years, raised two daughters, a half a dozen cats, and a few dogs. She was awarded a BA in English from the University of Tennessee and MFA in Writing from Vermont College. She is co-founder of the Chattanooga Writers Guild and leads their poetry group. Her poetry and translations have appeared in *The Louisville Review*, *The Southern Indiana Review*, *The Spoon River Poetry Review*, *Comstock Review*, *Eleventh Muse*, *Snake Nation Review*, *Voices International*, *Moebius*, *Free Focus*, *Phoenix*, *Quiddity*, among others, and several anthologies. Finishing Line Press published her chapbook *Wild Plums* in 2012. Blue Light Press published her full collection, *Luckier than the Stars*, in 2013.

W. F. LANTRY's poetry collections are *The Structure of Desire* (Little Red Tree 2012), winner of a 2013 Nautilus Award in Poetry, a chapbook, *The Language of Birds* (Finishing Line 2011), and a forthcoming collection *The Book of Maps*. Recent honors include the National Hackney Literary Award in Poetry, *CutBank* Patricia Goedicke Prize, *Crucible* Editors' Poetry Prize, Lindberg Foundation International Poetry for Peace Prize (in Israel), and in 2012 the LaNelle Daniel and *Potomac Review* Prizes. His work has appeared widely in publications such as *Atlanta Review*, *Descant*, *Gulf Coast* and *Aesthetica*. He is an associate fiction editor at *JMWW*. More at: http://wflantry.com.

MICHAEL LEVAN received his MFA in poetry from Western Michigan University and PhD in English and Creative Writing from the University of Tennessee. He is a Visiting Professor of English at the University of Saint Francis. His work can be found in recent or forthcoming issues of *Natural Bridge*, *Mid-American Review*, *American Literary Review*, and *New South*. He lives in Fort Wayne, Indiana, with his wife, Molly, and son, Atticus.

Born in Snowflake, Virginia, JUDY LOEST earned her Master's degree in English from the University of Tennessee in 1998. Her poetry has appeared in such journals as *Now & Then, The Cortland Review, New Millennium Writings,* and *storySouth,* and in The Poetry Society of America's *Poetry in Motion* program. Her nonfiction has been published in *EvaMag, France Magazine,* and *Metropulse.* Her awards include the Libba Moore Gray Poetry Prize, the James Still Poetry Award, and the Olay/Poetry Society of America Fine Lines Poetry Prize. She is editor of *Knoxville Bound,* a literary anthology inspired by Knoxville, Tennessee. Her poetry chapbook, *After Appalachia,* was published by Finishing Line Press in 2007; the poem "Faith" from that collection appeared in Ted Kooser's "American Life in Poetry" newspaper column in 2009.

DENTON LOVING lives on a farm near the historic Cumberland Gap, where Tennessee, Kentucky, and Virginia come together. He works at Lincoln Memorial University, where he co-directs the annual Mountain Heritage Literary Festival and serves as executive editor of *drafthorse: the literary journal of work and no work.* His poem "Reasoning with Cows" received first place in the 2012 Byron Herbert Reece Society poetry contest. Other fiction, poetry, and reviews have appeared in *Appalachian Heritage, Cosmos, Literal Latte, Main Street Rag,* and in numerous anthologies including *Degrees of Elevation: Stories of Contemporary Appalachia.*

JACQUELYN MALONE was born in Diana, Tennessee, and went to high school in Nashville. She has been a recipient of a National Endowment for the Arts Fellowship grant in poetry. Her work has appeared in *Poetry Magazine, Beloit Poetry Journal, Cimarron Review, Cortland Review, Cumberland Review, Ploughshares,* and *Poetry Northwest.* The poem published in the *Beloit Journal* was nominated for the Pushcart Prize. She is the writer/editor for masspoetry.org, the site for the Massachusetts Poetry Festival. Finishing Line Press published her chapbook *All Waters Run to Lethe* in 2011.

MICHAEL O. MARBERRY's work has appeared or is forthcoming in *The New Republic, Verse Daily, Indiana Review, Third Coast, Guernica, Linebreak, Anti-,* and elsewhere. A graduate of The Ohio State University, the University of Alabama, and Lipscomb University, Michael is now a PhD student at Western Michigan University.

JEFF DANIEL MARION has published nine poetry collections, four poetry chapbooks, and a children's book. His poems have appeared in *The Southern Review, Southern Poetry Review, Shenandoah, Atlanta Review, Tar River Poetry,* and many others. In 1978, Marion received the first Literary Fellowship awarded by the Tennessee Arts Commission. *Ebbing & Flowing Springs: New and Selected Poems and Prose, 1976-2001* won the 2003 Independent Publisher Award in Poetry and was named Appalachian Book of the Year by the Appalachian Writers Association. His collection *Father* received the 2009 Quentin R. Howard Poetry Prize, and in 2011 he was awarded the James Still Award for Writing about the Appalachian South by the Fellowship of Southern Writers. Marion served as the Jack E. Reese Writer-in-Residence for the University of Tennessee Libraries, Knoxville, from 2009-2011. In spring 2013, his work and career were celebrated at Carson-Newman University and Walters State Community College.

LINDA PARSONS MARION is an editor at the University of Tennessee and the author of three poetry collections, most recently, *Bound.* She served as poetry editor of *Now & Then* magazine for many years and has received literary fellowships from the Tennessee Arts Commission, as well as the Associated Writing Programs' Intro Award and the 2012 George

Scarbrough Award in Poetry, among others. Marion's work has appeared in journals such as *The Georgia Review, Iowa Review, Poet Lore, Asheville Poetry Review, Shenandoah, Louisiana Literature, Birmingham Poetry Review,* and Ted Kooser's syndicated column *American Life in Poetry* and in numerous anthologies, including *Listen Here: Women Writing in Appalachia* and *The Southern Poetry Anthology, Volume III: Contemporary Appalachia.*

CLAY MATTHEWS has recent work published or forthcoming in *The American Poetry Review, Blackbird, The Kenyon Review, Southern Humanities Review,* and elsewhere. He is the author of three books of poetry: *Superfecta* (Ghost Road Press), *Runoff* (BlazeVOX Books), and *Pretty, Rooster* (Cooper Dillon Books). He teaches at The Tusculum College in East Tennessee and works as a poetry editor for *The Tusculum Review.*

ANDREW MCFADYEN-KETCHUM's first book of poems, *Ghost Gear,* is forthcoming in 2014 with the University of Arkansas Press; his anthology, *Apocalypse Now: Poems and Prose from the End of Days,* was released in 2012. He is Founder and Editor of PoemoftheWeek.org; is Acquisitions Editor for Upper Rubber Boot Books; writes a web-column, "Poetry=AndrewM^K" for *Southern Indiana Review;* is a consultant for Wolfram Productions; and teaches writing at Metro State University of Denver. McFadyen-Ketchum's work recently appears or is forthcoming in journals such as *The Writer's Chronicle, Blackbird, Ascent, Glimmer Train, Iron Horse, American Literary Review, The Spoon River Poetry Review, Poet Lore, The Missouri Review, storySouth, InsideHigherEd.com, Eclipse, Copper Nickel, New Letters, Hayden's Ferry Review,* and *Potomac Review,* among others. Read his work at www. AndrewMK.com.

ANNE MEEK serves as president of the Cultural Alliance of Greater Hampton Roads and an advisor to the board of the Hampton Roads Writers. You can find her recent poetry in *The Poet's Domain* and *Skipping Stones* and her creative nonfiction in *In Good Company.* When she lived in Tennessee (Martin, Memphis, and Knoxville), Anne's poems appeared in *Tennessee Poetry Journal, The Small Farm, The Phoenix, Plainsong, Windless Orchard, Phi Delta Kappan,* and *Educational Catalyst.* During her career in education, Anne edited *Tennessee Educational Leadership* and served as managing editor of *Educational Leadership.* At present, she is editing a book on the school dropout problem for a grad school colleague with a University of Tennessee doctorate; drafting a Southern Gothic novella, *Mother Knows Best;* and looking for an agent to market her novel manuscript, "Trash Can Posies."

ELIJAH RENE MENDOZA is a Mexican-American poet who was born in the South. He has graduated from Vanderbilt University and the University of California, Riverside, and taught in the English Departments of Baylor University and Tarrant County College. Mendoza enjoys the South because of its complexities and would like to call attention to the region as rapidly evolving and progressing through the twenty-first century.

JOANNE MERRIAM is the author of *The Glaze from Breaking* (Stride, 2005) and runs Upper Rubber Boot Books. She lives in Nashville.

COREY MESLER has published in numerous journals and anthologies. He has published seven novels, three full-length poetry collections, and three books of short stories. He has also published a dozen chapbooks of both poetry and prose. He has been nominated for the Pushcart Prize numerous times, and two of his poems were chosen for Garrison Keillor's Writer's Almanac. His fiction has received praise from John Grisham, Robert Olen Butler,

Lee Smith, Frederick Barthelme, Greil Marcus, among others. With his wife, he runs Burke's Book Store in Memphis, Tennessee. He can be found at www.coreymesler.wordpress.com.

BEVERLY ACUFF MOMOI's poems have been published widely, appearing in such journals as *Acorn, A Hundred Gourds, American Tanka, Eucalypt, Frogpond, Modern Haiku, River Styx, Ribbons, Simply Haiku,* and *Spillway.* They have also appeared in the anthologies, *Looking for Home: Women Writing About Exile, The Party Train: A Collection of North American Prose Poetry,* and *Take Five: Best Contemporary Tanka, Volume 4.* Her haibun collection, *Lifting the Towhee's Song,* was a 2011 Snapshot Press eChapbook Award winner and is freely available online at: http://www.snapshotpress.co.uk/ebooks.htm.

R. B. MORRIS is a poet and songwriter, solo performer and bandleader, and a sometimes playwright and actor from Knoxville, Tennessee. He has published books of poetry, including *Early Fires* (Iris Press) and *Keeping the Bees Employed* (Rich Mountain Bound), and music albums including *Spies Lies and Burning Eyes* and his most recent solo project *Rich Mountain Bound.* He wrote and acted in *The Man Who Lives Here Is Loony,* a one-man play taken from the life and work of writer James Agee, and was instrumental in founding a park dedicated to Agee in Knoxville. Morris served as the Jack E. Reese Writer-in-Residence at the University of Tennessee from 2004-2008, and he was inducted into the East Tennessee Writers Hall of Fame in 2009. He lives in Knoxville.

KEVIN E. O'DONNELL teaches composition and literature at East Tennessee State University, in Johnson City.

TED OLSON has published two book-length collections of poetry, *Revelations* (Celtic Cat Publishing, 2012) and *Breathing in Darkness* (Wind Publications, 2006). He is also the author of a scholarly book, *Blue Ridge Folklife* (University Press of Mississippi, 1998), the editor of collections of literary work by such authors as James Still, Sarah Orne Jewett, and Sherwood Anderson, as well as the co-editor of several compilations of Tennessee-based or Appalachia-based scholarship, including *A Tennessee Folklore Sampler* (University of Tennessee Press, 2009) and *The Bristol Sessions: Writings About the Big Bang of Country Music* (McFarland & Co., Inc., Publishers, 2005). A recipient of three Grammy Award nominations for his work as a music historian, Olson teaches in East Tennessee State University's Department of Appalachian Studies and in East Tennessee State University's Bluegrass, Old-Time, and Country Music Program.

WILLIAM PAGE's poems have appeared widely in such journals as *North American Review, The Southern Review, Southwest Review, Sewanee Review, Southern Poetry Review, Valparaiso Poetry Review, Rattle, Ploughshares, Literary Review, American Literary Review, Mississippi Review, Kansas Quarterly, Wisconsin Review, South Carolina Review, Chariton Review, Rosebud, Pedestal Magazine,* and in a number of print and online anthologies, including *Enskyment.* His third volume of poems, *Bodies Not Our Own* (Memphis State University Press), was awarded a Walter R. Smith Distinguished Book Award. His collection *William Page's Greatest Hits: 1970-2000* is from Pudding House Publications. He was Founding Editor of *The Pinch* and is a retired member of the Creative Writing Faculty at the University of Memphis.

RANDY PARKER is a freelance marketing and advertising writer in Memphis and a graduate of the University of Memphis' creative writing program. His work has appeared in *Grey Sparrow, Tidal Basin Review, Avatar Review, Barely South*, and many other publications. This is his first appearance in an anthology.

CHARLOTTE PENCE's full-length poetry collection, *Spike*, will be released by Black Lawrence Press in 2014. She is also the author of two award-winning poetry chapbooks, *The Branches, the Axe, the Missing* (Black Lawrence Press, 2012) and *Weaves a Clear Night* (Flying Trout Press, 2011). Pence also edited *The Poetics of American Song Lyrics* (University Press of Mississippi, 2012) that explores the similarities and differences between poetry and songs. She is a professor at Eastern Illinois University.

EMILIA PHILLIPS is the author of *Signaletics* (University of Akron Press, August 2013) and two chapbooks. Her poetry appears in *AGNI, Beloit Poetry Journal, Green Mountains Review, Gulf Coast, Hayden's Ferry Review, Indiana Review, The Journal, The Kenyon Review, Narrative, The Paris-American, Third Coast*, and elsewhere. She's the recipient of the 2012 Poetry Prize from *The Journal*, selected by G. C. Waldrep; 2nd Place in *Narrative*'s 2012 30 Below Contest; and fellowships from US Poets in Mexico, Vermont Studio Center, and Virginia Commonwealth University. She serves as the prose editor for *32 Poems* and teaches poetry at Virginia Commonwealth University. She is the 2013–2014 Emerging Writer Lecturer at Gettysburg College.

DAVID S. POINTER currently resides in Murfreesboro, Tennessee. Recent publications include *Rattle, Popshot, Stone Canoe*, and *Proud to Be: Writing by American Warriors*. Pointer's most recent book is entitled *Oncoming Crime Facts*. He serves on the advisory panel at "Writing for Peace." Moreover, Pointer teaches sociology online at Columbia State Community College in Columbia, Tennessee.

MICHAEL POTTS is Professor of Philosophy, Methodist University, Fayetteville, North Carolina. A native of Smyrna, Tennessee, and a 1980 graduate of Smyrna High School, he holds the BA degree from David Lipscomb University, the MTh from Harding University Graduate School of Religion, the MA from Vanderbilt University, and he received his Ph.D. in philosophy from The University of Georgia in 1992. His poetry has been published in *Bay Leaves, Iodine Poetry Journal, Journal of the American Medical Association, Old Red Kimono, Pinesong Awards, Poem, Poems & Plays, The Mid-America Poetry Review*, and *The Penwood Review*. His chapbook, *From Field to Thicket*, won the 2006 Mary Belle Campbell Poetry Book Award of the North Carolina Writers Network. He is a 2007 graduate of MTSU's Writer's Loft program. He and his wife, Karen, and their three cats live in Linden, North Carolina.

LYNN POWELL is the author of two books of poetry, *Old & New Testaments* and *The Zones of Paradise*, and a book of non-fiction, *Framing Innocence: A Mother's Photographs, a Prosecutor's Zeal, and a Small Town's Response*. She has received fellowships from the Ohio Arts Council and the National Endowment for the Arts, and her poems have been included in numerous anthologies, including *180 More: Extraordinary Poems for Everyday* and the most recent edition of *The Norton Introduction to Literature*. Born, raised, and educated in East Tennessee, Powell now lives with her family in Oberlin, Ohio.

MELISSA RANGE's first book of poems, *Horse and Rider* (Texas Tech University Press, 2010), won the 2010 Walt McDonald Prize in Poetry. Range is the recipient of a Rona

Jaffe Foundation Writers' Award, a "Discovery"/*The Nation* prize, and fellowships from the American Antiquarian Society, Yaddo, the Virginia Center for Creative Arts, the Sewanee Writers' Conference, and the Fine Arts Work Center in Provincetown. Her poems have appeared in *32 Poems, The Georgia Review, The Hudson Review, Image, New England Review, The Paris Review,* and other journals. Originally from Elizabethton, Tennessee, she's finishing up her PhD in English at the University of Missouri.

SAM RASNAKE's works, receiving five nominations for the Pushcart Prize, have appeared in *MiPOesias Companion 2012, Best of the Web 2009, Wigleaf, OCHO, Poem, Big Muddy, Literal Latté, Poets/Artists, Santa Fe Literary Review, LUMMOX 2012, BOXCAR Poetry Review Anthology 2,* and *Dogzplot Flash Fiction 2011.* He is chapbook editor for *Sow's Ear Poetry Review* and has served as a judge for the Dorothy Sargent Rosenberg Poetry Prize, University of California, Berkeley, and from 2001-2010 was editor of *Blue Fifth Review.* Since 2011, Rasnake has edited, along with Michelle Elvy, the *Blue Five Notebook Series* from BFR. His latest poetry collection, *Cinéma Vérité,* is forthcoming (Autumn 2013) from A-Minor Press.

ANNE DELANA REEVES lives, works, and writes in Columbia, Tennessee. Her poems have appeared in *The Antioch Review, Indiana Review, Image,* and the *Nashville Scene.* Her poem "The Hands of Ché Guevara" was chosen for the international anthology, *Ché In Verse.* Her essays and book reviews appear regularly in *Chapter 16.org, Humanities Tennessee Online Council.* She has spent a few fortunate years as a songwriter in Nashville; her songs have been recorded by Lee Ann Womack, LeAnn Rimes, and Farmer's Daughter (Canada), among other artists. She spends her free time writing and wandering with her two dogs Seamus and Angus. Reeves is Tutor Coordinator for Columbia State Community College in Columbia, Tennessee.

Poems by J. STEPHEN RHODES have appeared in *Shenandoah, Tar River Poetry,* and *The International Poetry Review,* among others. His poetry collection, *The Time I Didn't Know What to Do Next,* was recently published by Wind Publications. He holds an MFA from the University of Southern Maine, Stonecoast, and a PhD in theology from Emory University. From 1988-1993 he served as the Academic Dean of Memphis Theological Seminary, and he continues to enjoy hiking in the Great Smoky Mountains National Park.

JOSHUA ROBBINS is the author of *Praise Nothing* (University of Arkansas Press, 2013). His recognitions include the James Wright Poetry Award, the *New South* Prize, and selection for the *Best New Poets* anthology. He is Visiting Assistant Professor of English at the University of the Incarnate Word, where he teaches creative writing and literature. He lives in San Antonio.

KRISTIN ROBERTSON was raised in Chattanooga and attended the University of Tennessee in Knoxville, and now she teaches at Maryville College. Her work has appeared recently in *Alaska Quarterly Review, Smartish Pace, Greensboro Review, Mid-American Review, Crab Orchard Review,* and on *Verse Daily.*

BOBBY C. ROGERS is Professor of English and Writer-in-Residence at Union University in Jackson, Tennessee. His book *Paper Anniversary* won the Agnes Lynch Starrett Poetry Prize at the University of Pittsburgh Press, was nominated for the Poets' Prize, and received the Lilly Fellows Program in Humanities and the Arts' 2012 Arlin G. Meyer Prize in Imaginative Writing.

LISA RONEY still feels her roots in her birth town of Memphis, Tennessee, though the frontier habits of her forebears have influenced her as well. She has also lived in Knoxville; Northfield and St. Paul, Minnesota; State College, Pennsylvania; Seattle, Washington; and Orlando, Florida, all of which inhabit her writing as she has inhabited them. She is associate professor of English at the University of Central Florida. Her poetry, fiction, and nonfiction has been included in *Harper's, Sycamore Review, Red Rock Review, So to Speak, the new renaissance, Ruminate, Hiram Poetry Review, The Healing Muse, Saw Palm, Numéro Cinq,* and *storySouth,* among others. She is the author of *Sweet Invisible Body: Reflections on a Life with Diabetes,* is finishing up a book on creative writing for Oxford University Press, and is working on a family history of marriage.

JANE SASSER's writing has appeared in *The Sun, The Atlanta Review, North American Review, Appalachian Heritage,* and other anthologies and publications. She has published two poetry chapbooks, *Recollecting the Snow* and *Itinerant.* She lives in Oak Ridge, Tennessee, with her husband, George, and rescue greyhounds.

JAMES SCRUTON is the author of four collections of poems, including the prize-winning chapbooks *Galileo's House* (Finishing Line Press, 2004), and *Exotics and Accidentals* (Grayson Books, 2009). He has received the Frederick Bock Prize from *Poetry* and the Dale Goodwin Poetry Award, among other honors. He lives on a farm outside McKenzie, Tennessee.

Connecticut State University Distinguished Professor, VIVIAN SHIPLEY teaches at Southern Connecticut State University. Her ninth book, *All of Your Messages Have Been Erased* (Southeastern Louisiana University, 2010), was nominated for the Pulitzer Prize, received the Paterson Prize for Sustained Literary Achievement, NEPC's Sheila Motton Book Prize, and the Connecticut Press Club Prize for Best Creative Writing. *Greatest Hits: 1974-2010* (Pudding House Press, Youngstown, Ohio, 2010) is her sixth chapbook. She has received the Library of Congress's Connecticut Lifetime Achievement Award for Service to the Literary Community and the Connecticut Book Award for Poetry. Other poetry awards include the Poetry Society of America's Lucille Medwick Prize, Robert Frost Foundation Poetry Prize, Ann Stanford Poetry Prize from University of Southern California, Marble Faun Poetry Prize from William Faulkner Society, NEPC's Daniel Varoujan Prize and the Hart Crane Prize from Kent State. Raised in Kentucky, a member of the University of Kentucky Hall of Distinguished Alumni, she has a PhD from Vanderbilt University.

ARTHUR SMITH's first book of poems, *Elegy on Independence Day,* was awarded the Agnes Lynch Starrett Poetry Prize and was selected by the Poetry Society of American to receive the Norma Farber First Book Award. He is the author of three other collections of poetry: *Orders of Affection, The Late World,* and *The Fortunate Era.* His work has been honored with a "Discovery"/The Nation Award, a National Endowment for the Arts Creative Writing Fellowship, two Pushcart Prizes, and he was selected as the Theodore Morrison Fellow in Poetry for the 1987 Bread Loaf Writer's Conference. He served two terms as an advisory member of the Tennessee Arts Commission Literary Panel, and he is Professor of English at the University of Tennessee.

JAMES MALONE SMITH's poems appear in *AGNI* (online), *Atlanta Review, Connecticut Review, Nebraska Review, Poet Lore, Prairie Schooner, Quarterly West, Shenandoah, Tar River Poetry* and others. His fiction has appeared in *American Short Fiction.* He is the co-editor of *Southern Poetry Review,* as well as the editor of the anthology *Don't Leave Hungry: Fifty Years of Southern Poetry Review* (University of Arkansas Press, 2009). Smith is Professor of English at Armstrong Atlantic State University in Savannah, Georgia, where he teaches creative writing and American literature. He grew up in the mountain of north Georgia and western North Carolina and attended Young Harris College. He went on to complete his BA degree at Berry College and then the MA and PhD at Vanderbilt University.

STEVE SPARKS lived for sixteen years in east Tennessee, formerly from north Alabama. He was a lecturer in the English Department at the University of Tennessee, Knoxville. His poetry was published in *North American Review, Number One, New Millennium Writings, Now & Then,* and in *The Southern Poetry Anthology, Volume III: Contemporary Appalachia.* Steve Sparks passed away in Knoxville, July 2013.

DAVID STALLINGS was born in the US South, raised in Alaska and Colorado before settling in the Pacific Northwest. Once an academic geographer, he has long worked to promote public transportation in the Puget Sound area. His poems have appeared in several North American and UK literary journals and anthologies, and in *Resurrection Bay,* a recent chapbook.

DARIUS STEWART was born in 1979 and grew up in Knoxville, Tennessee. He attended Tennessee State University and The University of Tennessee, where he earned a BA with honors in English. He is a former fellow of the Bucknell Seminar for Younger Poets and the Michener Center for Writers at the University of Texas-Austin, where he graduated with an MFA in poetry. His poems have appeared in *Appalachian Heritage, Callaloo, The Seattle Review, Meridian, Poet Lore, Verse Daily,* and *The Southern Poetry Anthology, Volume III: Contemporary Appalachia,* among various other journals and anthologies. He is the author of two chapbooks published in the Main Street Rag Chapbook Series: *The Terribly Beautiful* (2006) and *Sotto Voce* (2008).

LARRY D. THACKER serves as Associate Dean of Students at Lincoln Memorial University near his hometown of Middlesboro, Kentucky. A seventh-generation Cumberland Gap area native, his creative interests include poetry, short stories, painting, and photography. Author of *Mountain Mysteries: The Mystic Traditions of Appalachia* and *Voice Hunting,* his work has been included in *Appalachian Heritage, Still: The Journal, Motif 2, The Emancipator,* and *Full of Crow.*

KEVIN THOMASON is from Memphis, Tennessee. He graduated from the University of Memphis in 2008 with degrees in English and History and is currently a student in the MFA program at McNeese State University in Lake Charles, Louisiana.

SUSAN O'DELL UNDERWOOD is Director of Creative Writing at Carson-Newman University in Jefferson City, Tennessee, where she also teaches Appalachian literature and poetry. She has an MFA from the University of North Carolina at Greensboro and a PhD from Florida State University. Her poetry, essays, and short fiction have been published in a number of journals and anthologies, and a chapbook of poetry, *From,* was published in 2010. She's married to artist David Underwood.

KORY WELLS grew up on the stories of her southern Appalachian family and the wonder of the Space Age, diverse influences that have shaped her life's work and writing. Author of the poetry chapbook *Heaven Was the Moon* (March Street Press), she often performs her poetry with her daughter Kelsey, an Appalachian old-time musician. The duo released their spoken word and roots music album *Decent Pan of Cornbread* in 2012. Kory's novel-in-progress was a William Faulkner competition finalist, and her "standout" nonfiction has been praised by *Ladies' Home Journal*. Her work appears in *Christian Science Monitor, Ruminate, Deep South Magazine, Now & Then*, and other publications. A longtime resident of Murfreesboro, Tennessee, Kory works in technology and is also a mentor with The Writer's Loft at Middle Tennessee State University. http://korywells.com

DANIEL WESTOVER grew up by turns in California, Utah, Idaho, Oregon, and Pennsylvania. He holds a PhD from the University of Wales and an MFA from McNeese State University. His books include *R.S. Thomas: A Stylistic Biography* (University of Wales Press, 2011), a literary biography of the great Welsh priest-poet; *Toward Omega* (21st Editions, 2005), a poetry/photography collaboration with Vincent Serbin; and the forthcoming *Leslie Norris: A Ghost Story* (Parthian, 2015), a biography of the Welsh poet and short story writer. He is also co-editing (with William Wright) *The World Is Charged: Poetic Engagements with Gerard Manley Hopkins*. Westover's poems have appeared in *North American Review, Crab Orchard Review, Southeast Review, Spoon River Poetry Review, Tar River Poetry, Asheville Poetry Review*, and *Measure*, as well as in *Poems of Devotion: An Anthology of Recent Poets* (2012). He lives with his wife Mary and their two daughters in Johnson City, Tennessee, where he is Assistant Professor of English at East Tennessee State University.

JOE WILKINS is the author of a memoir, *The Mountain and the Fathers: Growing Up on the Big Dry*, a Montana Book Award Honor Book and a finalist for the *Orion* Book Award, and two collections of poems, *Notes from the Journey Westward*, winner of the White Pine Press Poetry Prize, and *Killing the Murnion Dogs*, a finalist for the Paterson Poetry Prize and the High Plains Book Award. Wilkins's poems, essays, and stories have appeared in *The Georgia Review, The Southern Review, Ecotone, The Sun, Orion*, and *Slate*, among other magazines and literary journals. A finalist for the National Magazine Award and the PEN Center USA Award, Wilkins now lives with his wife, son, and daughter in western Oregon, where he teaches writing at Linfield College.

CLAUDE WILKINSON's poems have appeared in numerous journals and anthologies. His first poetry collection, *Reading the Earth*, won the Naomi Long Madgett Poetry Award. In 2000, Wilkinson became the first poet to be chosen as the John and Renee Grisham Visiting Southern Writer in Residence at the University of Mississippi. He also received the Whiting Writers' Award. His book, *Joy in the Morning*, was nominated for a Pulitzer Prize in 2005. In addition to poetry, he has published literary criticism on such diverse writers as Chinua Achebe, Italo Calvino, and John Cheever. Also a visual artist, his paintings have been featured in exhibitions at Bennington Center for the Arts, Carter House Gallery, Southside Gallery, Tennessee Valley Art Center, and University Museums, among many other invitational, juried, and solo shows.

SYLVIA WOODS lives in Oak Ridge, Tennessee, where she teaches high school English. Her work has appeared in various magazines and anthologies including *Appalachian Heritage, Motif*, and *The Southern Poetry Anthology, Volume III: Contemporary Appalachia*.

MARIANNE WORTHINGTON grew up in the Fountain City neighborhood in Knoxville, Tennessee. She is co-founder and poetry editor of the online literary journal *Still: The Journal* and poetry editor for *Now & Then: The Appalachian Magazine*. Her poetry chapbook, *Larger Bodies than Mine* (Finishing Line Press), won the Appalachian Book of the Year Award in Poetry. Her poems, essays, reviews, and feature articles have appeared widely and in several anthologies including *Knoxville Bound*, *Cornbread Nation 5*, and The *Southern Poetry Anthology, Volume III: Contemporary Appalachia*. She is a recipient of the Al Smith Fellowship from the Kentucky Arts Council and has lived in Williamsburg, Kentucky, since 1990.

AMY WRIGHT is the Nonfiction Editor of *Zone 3 Press* and *Zone 3* journal, as well as the author of three chapbooks—*Farm*, *There Are No New Ways to Kill a Man*, and *The Garden Will Give You a Fat Lip*. She was awarded a 2012 fellowship for the Kenyon Review Writers Workshop and has been recognized for excellence in teaching.

CHARLES WRIGHT was born in Pickwick Dam, Tennessee, in 1935 and was educated at Davidson College and the University of Iowa. His books include *Sestets: Poems* (Farrar, Straus and Giroux, 2010); *Littlefoot: A Poem* (2008); *Scar Tissue* (2007), which was the international winner for the Griffin Poetry Prize; *Buffalo Yoga* (Farrar, Straus & Giroux, 2004); *Negative Blue* (2000); *Appalachia* (1998); *Black Zodiac* (1997), which won the Pulitzer Prize and the Los Angeles Times Bok Prize, *Chickamauga* (1995), which won the 1996 Lenore Marshall Poetry Prize; *The World of the Ten Thousand Things: Poems 1980-1990; Zone Journals* (1988); *Country Music: Selected Early Poems* (1983), which won the National Book Award; *Hard Freight* (1973), which was nominated for the National Book Award, among others. He has also written two volumes of criticism and has translated the work of Dino Campana in *Orphic Songs* as well as Eugenio Montale's *The Storms and Other Poems*, which was awarded the PEN Translation Prize. He is Souder Family Professor of English at the University of Virginia in Charlottesville.

BRENDA YATES is from nowhere. After growing up in Tennessee, Delaware, Florida, Michigan, Massachusetts, Japan, and Hawaii, mostly on SAC bases stateside and overseas, she settled first in Massachusetts and finally (so far) in California. Her poems have appeared in *Mississippi Review, Eclipse, Pearl, In Posse Review, 51%, Haywire, Cider Press Review, Spillway, Blue Arc West, So Luminous the Wildflowers: An Anthology of California Poets*, and *Don't Blame the Ugly Mug: Two Idiots Peddling Poetry*. Honors include a 2010 Pushcart nomination, The 2010 Beyond Baroque Poetry Prize, and the Patricia Bibby Memorial Scholarship at Idyllwild Arts.

RAY ZIMMERMAN is the editor of *Southern Light: Twelve Contemporary Southern Poets*. His poem "Glen Falls Trail" won second place in the Tennessee Writers Alliance poetry contest (2007). Finishing Line Press of Georgetown, Kentucky, released his chapbook *First Days* in February of 2013. His poems have also appeared in *2nd and Church* magazine, Nashville, *Soundtrack not Included* anthology, Nashville Writers Meetup, and the *Tapestry of Voices* anthology, Knoxville Writers Guild. The Trenton Arts Council of Trenton, Georgia, included his poems in their *Presenting the Beatniks* anthology, *The Beatniks Are Back* video disc, and their *Appalachia Rising* CD. He has served two terms of president of the Chattanooga Writers Guild.

Acknowledgements

For contributors who supplied publication information, details are listed below. All poem copyrights have reverted back to respective authors, listed or otherwise, and Texas Review Press has permission to reprint poems included herein.

The editors would like to thank Jeff Daniel Marion, Thomas Alan Holmes, and Catherine Pritchard Childress for their significant help with this anthology.

DARNELL ARNOULT: "Lining Out" appeared in *Appalachian Heritage*.

BETH BACHMANN: "Temper" and "Elegy" appear in *Temper* (2009) and are reprinted in this anthology with permission from the University of Pittsburgh Press.

JEFF BAKER: "At Chota" appeared in *Copper Nickel*.

EVELYN MCAMIS BALES: "All That Remains" appeared in *A! Magazine for the Arts*.

TINA BARR: "Hour of the Cardinals" appeared in *The Antioch Review*; "Guns Not for Sale" in *New South*.

DIANN BLAKLEY: "Hellhound on My Trail" appeared in *Oxford American*; "History" in *Farewell, My Lovelies* (Story Line Press, 2000).

BILL BROWN: "My Mother's Soul" appeared in *Rattle* and *Late Winter* (Iris Press, 2008); "And" in *Prairie Schooner* and *Late Winter* (Iris Press, 2008); "Long Division" in *Tar River Poetry* and *The News Inside* (Iris Press, 2010).

MELISSA CANNON: "The Vigil" appeared in *The Lyric*.

CATHERINE PRITCHARD CHILDRESS: "Putting Up Corn" appeared in *The Rectangle*.

GEORGE DAVID CLARK: "Matches" appeared in *Cimmaron Review*; "Lullaby with Perigee" in *Crab Orchard Review*.

JIM CLARK: "The Land under the Lake" appeared in *Handiwork* (St. Andrews College Press, 1998).

ENA DJORDJEVIC: "Unnamed Language" appeared in *Thesmokingpoet.com*.

LISA DORDAL: "Wedding" appeared in *Southern Women's Review*.

SUE WEAVER DUNLAP: "A Daughter's Homecoming" appeared in *Outscapes: Writings on*

Fences and Frontiers (2008).

RENEE EMERSON: "We Left Behind" appeared in *Existere.*

BLAS FALCONER: "Maybe I'm Not Here at All" appeared in *Luna;* "The Annunciation" in *Crab Orchard Review.*

LEA GRAHAM: "Crush Starting with a Line from Jack Gilbert" appeared in *Notre Dame Review.*

JESSE GRAVES: "The Kingdom of the Dead" appeared in *The Missouri Review Online;* "Cinnamon" in *Appalachian Journal.*

CONNIE JORDAN GREEN: "Regret Comes to Tea, Spends the Night" appeared in *Regret Comes to Tea, Spends the Night* (Finishing Line Press).

RASMA HAIDRI: "Lottery" appeared in *Prairie Schooner.*

PATRICIA HAMILTON: "Day of the Dead" appeared in *Off the Coast.*

KAY HECK: "Awakening Day" appeared in *Outscape: Writings on Fences and Frontiers* (Knoxville Writer's Guild, 2008).

GRAHAM HILLARD: "Lizard" appeared in *Tar River Poetry;* "What the Ground Gives" in *Reading Arts and Letter* and *Best New Poets 2010.*

RICK HILLES: "Missoula Eclipse" appeared in *Columbia Poetry Review;* "From Three Words of a Magnetic Poetry Set Found Caked in Dirt beneath James Merrill's Last Refrigerator" in *Blackbird;* "Larry Levis in Provincetown" in *Columbia Magazine.*

ANGIE HOGAN: "Apologia at Clinchfield Yards" appeared in *Threepenny Review;* "Lodge No. 422, Bulls Gap, TN" in *Third Coast.*

THOMAS ALAN HOLMES: "Mandolin" appeared in *The Connecticut Review;* "Jones Valley" in *Louisiana Literature.*

SCOTT C. HOLSTAD: "5th Avenue Motel" appeared in *Main Street Rag.*

JANICE HORNBURG: "My Father's Room" appeared in *Lost State Voice II.*

ELIZABETH HOWARD: "Willow Withe" appeared in *The Comstock Review.*

T. J. JARRETT: "After Forty Days, Go Marry Again" appeared in *Beloit Poetry Journal.*

DON JOHNSON: "The Importance of Visible Scars" appeared in *The Importance of Visible*

Scars (Wampeter Press, 1984) and *Here and Gone: New & Selected Poems* (Louisiana Literature Press, 2009); "The Russian Church at Ninilchik" in *Kaimana*.

MARILYN KALLET: "Cons" appeared in *Medulla Review* and *The Love That Moves Me* (Commonwealth Books, Black Widow, 2013); "Storm Warning" in *New Millennium Writings* and *The Love That Moves Me* (Commonwealth Books, Black Widow, 2013); "The Love That Moves Me" in *Prairie Schooner* and *The Love That Moves Me* (Commonwealth Books, Black Widow, 2013).

W. F. LANTRY: "Williams Was Right" appeared in *The Tennessee Quarterly*.

MICHAEL LEVAN: "Walking through the Weeds off Number Ten" appeared in *Crab Orchard Review*.

LINDA PARSONS MARION: "Mac" appeared in *Bound* (Wind Publications, 2011); "Genealogy" in *Appalachian Journal*; "Wanderlust" in *Roanoke Review*.

ANDREW MCFADYEN-KETCHUM: "Corridor," appeared in *The Southern Indiana Review*.

ANNE MEEK: "October, Knoxville" appeared in *redpepper*.

JOANNE MERRIAM: "Larix laricina Anaphora" appeared in *Alba*.

WILLIAM PAGE: "Skating" appeared in *The Innisfree Poetry Journal*; "Madame Le Coeur" in *The North American Review*.

RANDY PARKER: "Leaving Us" appeared in *Tidal Basin Review*.

CHARLOTTE PENCE: "Yard Meditation" appeared in *Iron Horse Literary Review*.

EMILIA PHILLIPS: "Strange Meeting" appeared in *Strange Meeting* (Eureka Press, 2010); "Creation Myth" in *Asheville Poetry Review* and *Strange Meeting* (Eureka Press, 2010).

LYNN POWELL: "July's Proverb" appeared in *Riverdell*; "Original Errata" in *The Zones of Paradise*.

MELISSA RANGE: "High Lonesome" appeared in *The Georgia Review* and *Horse and Rider* (Texas Tech University Press, 2010).

SAM RASNAKE: "A Certainty and Not the Poem I Meant to Write" appeared in *Naugatuck River Review*; "Mountain Verse" in *The Dead Mule School of Southern Literature*.

JOSHUA ROBBINS: "Sparrow" appeared in *Sonora Review 57*.

KRISTIN ROBERTSON: "Bonfire" appeared in *Passages North*.

BOBBY C. ROGERS: "William Eggleston" appeared in *Image*; "Lost Highway" in *Shenandoah*

VIVIAN SHIPLEY "Praying you are asleep," and "Our bodies, arms of a weathervane pointing north and south" appeared in *Gleanings: Old Poems, New Poems* (Louisiana Literature Press, SLU, 2003).

JAMES MALONE SMITH: "Mandelshtam's Wonderful Window" appeared in *Shenandoah*.

DAVID STALLINGS: "Message" appeared in *Milk Money* and in *Resurrection Bay* (Evening Street Press).

DARIUS STEWART: "The Terribly Beautiful" and "Driftwood" appeared in *The Terribly Beautiful* (Main Street Rag, 2005).

KORY WELLS: "And This Will Be a Sign" appeared in *Christian Science Monitor*.

DANIEL WESTOVER: "Waiting at the Crossing" appeared in *Spoon River Poetry Review*.

CLAUDE WILKINSON: "Parable, Late October" appeared in *Joy in the Morning* (Louisiana State University Press, 2004).

SYLVIA WOODS: "Knowing" appeared in *Now & Then* and *Cornbread Nation*.

MARIANNE WORTHINGTON: "1116 N. 3rd Avenue, Knoxville, TN" appeared in *A Knoxville Christmas* (Greyhound Books, 2007).

BRENDA YATES: "Tennessee Jukebox" appeared in *Spillway* and *Don't Blame the Ugly Mug Anthology*.

RAY ZIMMERMAN: "Glen Falls Trail" appeared at *vinestreetpress.com*.